Mosaic:

Caribbean Short Fiction Collection

Barbara Paul-Emile

Professor of English
Maurice E. Goldman Distinguished Professor of Arts & Sciences
Department of English and Media Studies
Bentley University
2015

EUNOIA
PUBLISHING

Mosaic: Caribbean Short Fiction Collection
Barbara Paul-Emile

Copyright © 2015 Barbara Paul-Emile

Published by Eunoia Publishing
P.O. Box 2211, Fairfield, Iowa 52556
tel: 641-209-5000 • fax: 866-440-5234
web: www.1stworldpublishing.com

First Edition

LCCN: 2015936502
Softcover ISBN: 978-1-4218-3729-1
Hardcover ISBN: 978-1-4218-3730-7
eBook ISBN: 978-1-4218-3731-4

This material has been written and published for educational purposes to enhance one's well-being. In regard to health issues, the information is not intended as a substitute for appropriate care and advice from health professionals, nor does it equate to the assumption of medical or any other form of liability on the part of the publisher or author. The publisher and author shall have neither liability nor responsibility to any person or entity with respect to loss, damages, or injury claimed to be caused directly or indirectly by any information in this book.

For

beautiful

Oona and Maxine

Whose presence in my life

Is the source of endless joy and thanksgiving

From their Nana

Acknowledgements

I wish to express my gratitude to my husband, Serge, a warm generous-hearted man, and an indefatigable "multi-tasker," for his continued support of my writing program and for his loving assistance in bringing projects to completion.

I thank my daughter, Kimani Clarisse Paul-Emile, and her husband, Erin Vali, for their encouragement, loving support and their appreciation of island culture.

I offer thanks to my managing editor, Rodney Charles, who has been my mainstay during the publication process. He has been central to the creation of this collection of stories from its inception. Without his acceptance of this manuscript, professional guidance, caring advice, patience and visionary outlook, the publication of *Mosaic* might have remained a dream.

Bentley University is to be commended for its support of my creative writing program. I am pleased to state that I was granted sabbatical leave to complete this collection of stories. As an institution of higher learning, Bentley is to be recognized for the broad and generous support it offers faculty in advancing their work whether in research and scholarship and/or in Creative Writing.

I wish to remember and honor my Caribbean family members who have left me their legacy. To name a beloved few: my mother, Ivy Hillary; aunts and uncles: Delilah Hillary Jackson, Angie Hillary, Linda Hillary Gardner, Florence Taylor Stewart, Florence Ianthe Taylor, Phyllis and Maxwell Hillary, Lawrence Hillary, George Taylor; my sister, Constance Taylor King, and our father, Louis Beresford Taylor.

Modesta Hillary, aunt and surrogate parent, loved the Caribbean and taught me to honor and respect its culture and values. I offer gratitude for her guardianship, protection and loving kindness. Her support became the cornerstone of my life. From early childhood, she saw what I could become before I knew who I was.

I treasure the strong connection with members of my enormous family, many of whom share with me the experience of growing up in Jamaica. Conversations with these members, several of whom live abroad and still remain close, have kept family memories and island culture alive and vibrant, regardless of distance.

I think of my cousins: Errol "Toney" Hillary and his wife Mildred, Lurene Hillary Sambury, Stanley Hillary, Charlene Hillary Rice, Marjorie Hillary, Marie Taylor-Stewart and my nieces: Toni, Kerry-Ann and Leslie King. The stories, the anecdotes, the memories we share will live always in our hearts.

I wish to acknowledge the support I have received from

family members with roots in Haiti. I have benefited from their affection and their encouragement over the years. My mother-in-law, Louisine Prophète, personified her island and taught me its culture and cuisine. Dr. Edner and Dulia Prophète and family, Gemma Solimene, Jacques and Juliette Salomon, Renée Féquière, Dr. Marie-Carole Desrosiers, Eveline Paul-Emile, Alix and Jacqueline Paul-Emile, Harry Paul-Emile, Marie-Edith Coicou Cipolla, and Régine Coicou have enlarged my knowledge of Haitian traditions and have enriched my life in many ways.

I treasure the friendship of those whose presence in my life has deepened and nourished my own by their open hearts, loving spirit and their commitment to all that improves human life and build awareness of larger horizons for Caribbean people. I acknowledge Dr. Alix and Bernadette Cantave, Dr. Gerdes and Florienne Fleurant, Tazhmoye Venessa Crawford, Dr. Clifford Griffin.

Table of Content

Introduction

This collection presents stories that focus on the vicissitudes of daily life as experienced by people in small towns and rural districts in the Caribbean islands. Tales deal with personal dilemmas, class distinctions, psychic themes, and social issues as shaped by the legacy of colonialism and slavery and expressed in the complex heritage of the region.

These stories, in highlighting particular aspects of Caribbean society, explore attitudes towards parenting and child-rearing, relationships between males and females in romantic situations, roles played by both genders in family affairs and in society at-large and the place of the mystic, village *obeah woman* or *man*, as healer and mediator between the world of the living and of the dead.

These tales allow me to share with readers *the voices* of the characters that speak in my creative fiction, giving life to their actions, personalities, interests and priorities and presenting the dramas that punctuate their lives. *Mosaic* presents several of the different *faces* of the Caribbean as I have experienced, observed and envisioned them.

In travel brochures, glossy magazines, journals and TV commercials, the Caribbean is represented in beautiful color as a necklace of azure islands strung out in sparkling blue waters. The region is seen as a kind of paradise where happy and carefree people lead bucolic lives, joyous and pain-free. The main interest of the inhabitants is to dance, sing and to welcome and serve foreign visitors. The answer to pressing questions is always a smile and the response, *"No problem, man."*

In other media outlets, the image offered of the Caribbean is quite different and in many cases quite the opposite. Documentaries, socio-political and scholarly treatises present Caribbean societies as impoverished and lacking in the amenities that would make life productive and worthwhile: poor education for the majority, excessive violence and economic instability for all.

The professional middle class is often overlooked and towns and villages are shown to be places where people live in miserable conditions with little hope of improvement and no means of escape.

Neither image is entirely true or accurate. The experience of Caribbean and West Indian people is finely textured and multi-layered, shaped by complex strains of colonial history and contemporary circumstances that produce both tragedy and triumph. In the face of great population dislocation and the suffering inherent in the economic aftermath of slavery, these islanders have learned to survive against incredible odds.

The character of Caribbean people, described in broad strokes, is fascinating and thought-provoking. Resourceful, strikingly devoid of self-pity, Caribbean people are easy-going, quick to share their opinions and perspectives while rejecting victim mentality.

Resilient, enterprising and engaging, these open-hearted islanders exhibit an infectious sense of humor and good spirits. Gregarious and optimistic, most are always looking for that second, and occasionally, third or fourth chance in life.

Economically, times are, for the most part, very hard, indeed, and the road to success for many is non-extent. Yet, inherent self-confidence and belief in the ultimate benefi-cent running of the universe promotes and strengthens the will to survive and to prosper in difficult times.

Music in its various forms and rhythms is one of the life-lines of the region. Caribbean music, heavily influenced by African sources, is known the world over. Whether the forms are *Mento, Meringue, Compas, Salsa, Soca, Calypso or Reggae*, the provocative lyrics and evocative melodies backed by the hard-driving drums can be heard in cities and towns everywhere.

The visual arts and handicrafts, produced in Haiti and other islands, are sought after in international circles, and are among the holdings of some of the world's museums. Allowing for differences in languages, traditional Afri-can-based customs and the arts have always been a source of sustenance for Caribbean people and cut across class and racial lines – a shared legacy.

The creole cuisine of the Caribbean enjoyed by islanders and visitors alike is a fusion of African, East Asian and

European culinary traditions. The pepper-pot soups, ackee and cod fish, the pork griot, red beans and rice, curried goat, fried plantains, sweet potato pudding, jerk pork and chicken and the rum cakes nourish both body and spirit.

Spices such as thyme, mint and scotch bonnet peppers are relied on by cooks and are at the heart of the Caribbean meal. Well-prepared food is central to Caribbean culture and is a theme echoed in *Mosaic* as well.

Family is at the center of Caribbean life. Relationships are longlasting and deep. Family members, who live abroad seldom, if ever, forget their roots. Many return to visit, some to retire, but the majority offer economic support to sustain children and the elderly. Grandparents are central to this paradigm and serve as the communal safety net.

Indeed, the extended family plays a major role in strengthening the community, often paralleling the nuclear construction. It is commonplace for aunts, uncles and siblings to take the role of parents to the younger generation in times of need. Family connection has always been an important means of survival in the islands and those who have moved on ahead economically, are expected to reach back and assist those coming behind.

While much information has been disseminated about the Caribbean as a region for vacation travel, very little is known about the tenor of the lives of the people who live there.

Little is known of their cultural traditions; the ways in which reality is conceptualized and structured in such a way as to shape perspectives allowing islanders to survive and overcome challenges and to resolve issues in their daily lives.

Too little is known of the impact of the economic hardships that they face and the courage it takes to overcome. Little is known of the priorities that shape their values, personal and social, which in turn affect relationships creating the fabric of their society.

In what way does class affect private and public relationships? What is the role of the supernatural and other spiritual dimensions in people's lives? What are the core mythic beliefs that hold the social fabric together?

Mosaic explores several of these philosophical, social and psychological terrains in the stories it presents and shows Caribbean life in its panoply of colors.

How people respond to the vicissitudes of life is the stuff of literature: a literature that captures, refines, synthesizes and reflects the cultural richness and diversity of island life.

It is my intent, in this collection of tales to enter the homes, sit on the stones in the yard, be the unseen observer, hear the *voices*, listen to the conversations, capture the resonance of the culture and share my understanding that these islands are more than beautiful white, sandy beaches surrounded by a turquoise sea with a helpful and smiling wait-staff.

Caribbean life and culture is rich in history, custom and tradition shaped by a multiplicity of external and internal forces. Through the prism of literature, I seek to present the multi-layered and complex social relationships and frameworks that exist in Caribbean society and to uncover the dynamics that shape character and life-choices.

In a more intimate way, I wish to share my experience of the richness of island culture. The world of *Mosaic* and the characters that inhabit it are very well known to me for they live in my memory and in my heart. I was raised to share their vision, hopes and dreams. Caribbean culture shaped the principles and honed the values that have guided my life since childhood.

Lines that tell of shared past
and of origins ...
Words that tell of beginnings
and days gone by
when stories were links of days
strung out like leaves ...

Island Memories –
The Dance of Life: Poems for the Spirit

Barbara Paul-Emile Ph.D.

The Child

Nathan walked down the road in the cool of the afternoon, the gravel crackling under his feet. He was still wearing the loose navy over-shirt and dark pant tied to his waist by a sash which he had worn to work that day. His budjo bag hung over his slim shoulders, his machete swung in his hand.

Usually, he would be whistling to himself or talking to passersby, but not today. Today, he had things on his mind.

He walked at the edge of the road, nodding to friends and acquaintances or waving his machete in a friendly salute, but saying little. He did not look angry. He looked determined. Today, he meant to have it out with Ownie.

Today, she had to settle with him.

He turned off the road on to a narrow dirt path using his machete to brush the tall grass which threatened to obscure the way. The place wasn't kept up as it ought to be.

"They need a man around," he thought. His eyes passed over the land rich with banana and coconut trees and yam hills that were overgrown.

Lost in his own thoughts, he was hardly aware that he was approaching the grassy clearing which was the entrance to the large, brown, earthen yard. The smell of mint and the lemon trees planted at the edge of the compound focused his awareness.

The yard was bounded by three houses: one of a good size and two smaller ones. They were board houses, not thatched and at one time they had been painted. It was hard to make out their former colors now.

In the center of the yard was a large mango tree. As he approached, he recognized Miss Martie, the matriarch of the Thorpe family, sitting in her accustomed way, her back against the tree, her dress loosely wrapped around her thin body, her aged lined face a mask of knowing calm.

Nathan slowed as he came close to her and, stopping before he faced her, said "Good evening, Miss Martie Ma'am."

Martie looked up as though she was only now aware of him, and taking her pipe from between her lips said slowly, "How you do, Nathan?"

He did not respond because no response was necessary. She knew how he was. People believe that Martie knew everything. Word had it that she was a woman not to be fooled with. She was the wise one who could untangle the knots of life.

So he said to her, "I come to see Ownie, Ma'am."

She continued to puff away dreamily as he dropped

his bag and placed his machete carefully on top of it. He waited for her to speak.

Shifting his weight from one leg to the other, barely holding in his irritation, he continued, "So a whe Ownie is, Ma'am? I come fe see her."

Again, Martie did not answer right away, as though to dilute the combative energy she sensed emanating from him.

After a couple more slow puffs of her pipe she said: "Ownie is here and she is in her house. Why you no call her?"

Nathan knew which house was Ownie's and he knew that Dorret, Ownie's sister and Martie's other daughter, lived with Victor in the other house. They knew that he was familiar with the place. Very familiar.

Still, he had hoped for some help from Martie. Maybe she could make the way a little easier for him. He looked at her and knew that was not to be.

Then he would have to go into the house, Nathan thought.

He turned and began to walk toward the steps when he saw that Ownie had emerged and was watching him calmly from the veranda.

They looked at each other.

He said to her, "Me have fe talk to you."

She looked away and made no answer.

The sound of a whimpering baby came from within the

house. Dorret who was cooking the evening meal in the communal kitchen nearby put her head out the door and said aloud to Ownie, "A what mek you no want fe talk to Nathan?"

In the background Martie puffed meditatively on her pipe.

Nathan was not a big man. He was rather slender and wiry in his built. His skin, brown as the earth, showed his African and Scottish ancestry. Ownie had known him a long time.

Looking at him now she thought, "What is to happen between us now?"

She was tense but was not afraid.

She knew instinctively, however, that she had to mind how she went.

Should she remind him that she had warned him not to come? No, she would not do that.

Instead she said, attempting a disarming smile, "Nathan, no need for this, man, no need. You stoppin' by as you passin'?"

Nathan was standing near the steps and was now quite close to her.

Measuring his words he said, "Ownie why you treatin' me this way? A wha mek you want fe do dis?"

She did not respond at once, for they had been through this before. Many times before.

Finally, she said, "Me tell you already."

Nathan was a man with a temper which he often vented in curses. She knew that very well and expected a string of obscenities which would tell her how he felt. But he did not behave as expected.

He did not lose control.

Instead he said, "Wha you tell me is lies, Ownie. This is my child. *My child!* You hear me. *My Child!* You did tell me dat after it was born, for I was here."

Ownie cut her eyes, looked away and said sharply, "Me never tell you dat Nathan. Me never did. Me never say that the child was fe you. A you who want de child."

Shaken by the cutting coldness of her remarks, and feeling that being reasonable with her was getting him nowhere, Nathan shouted: "I am the fada to dis child. So a wha you guine do with me child?"

Ownie did not respond.

As the pitch of the voices rose, the baby in the house began to cry.

Swiftly, Ownie fled inside and picked up the child and returned with it to face Nathan. The presence of the child seemed to calm him.

He looked at both of them and repeated, "He is *my child!* You no want fe live with me in a regular way and you want fe tek me child!"

His words were bitter. He was not going to give way.

Something had to happen.

Ownie clung to the baby. She was not sure whether

she should put it down or continue to hold it. She looked around as though for help.

Dorret was still in the kitchen. Her mother was still puffing on her pipe and said nothing. No one had made a move to help her.

The tension was beginning to build. She did not dislike Nathan but what he wanted was permanence. She wasn't sure of that.

She liked her freedom. A woman needed to be free.

Carefully she placed the child down on a mat behind her, and turning to Nathan she said pleadingly, "Laud, man a wha mek you strong-headed so? Me say de pickney no fe you."

"So you want fe mek a fool of me. You mek me support the child from the beginning and now you want fe say different?"

She knew that there was no use repeating what had been said before. Yet it was as though Nathan had heard it anyway, for he responded, "So a wha guine happen Ownie?"

"Me no live a house with you Nathan, me do as me like. Me a free woman," said Ownie.

"No," said Nathan, "You a no-good woman, Ownie."

The look she gave him was one of cold indifference. She sucked her teeth, a sound made by forcing the breath out between clenched teeth, and cut her eyes away from him.

In a swift movement, he wheeled away, crossed the yard

and grasped his machete. Ownie felt cold and could not move. Dorret ran to the door of the kitchen.

But in a moment, Martie was in the center of the yard.

She had placed herself between Ownie and Nathan.

Looking at the young man as though willing him to be calm, she called him by his name and said, "Nathan, dis quarrel only guine cause trouble! Bad trouble! You know Ownie. You know how she own-way. Give me you machete. Mek me talk with her fe you. Mek me talk wid her, man." She paused and waited.

Nathan looked at the machete as though surprised to see it in his hand.

Martie took it from him.

With her low husky voice she spoke for his ears alone and said, "Nathan, a woman bear de child. Only she can decide. Dis not guine do no good. It is the way life is, man. You can't lay claim to a child like dat. I guine talk wid her fe you."

Her soothing words pulled the venom from the air, and she motioned him to sit on a large stone in the yard.

Still holding the machete for safe-keeping, Martie called to Ownie and together they went into the house. Nathan waited.

Time passed slowly.

Finally, Ownie emerged.

She was a slender woman, quick and graceful in her movements. Her bare feet made no sound on the earth as she moved.

She reached Nathan and, standing next to him, she bent and picked up a stone from the yard, held it loosely in her hand and contemplated it slowly.

The air lay heavy between them. What Martie had said to Ownie, Nathan could not tell, but he knew that a river had been crossed and a decision had been made.

Turning to her he said quietly, "Ownie, a what mek you won't give me my child? Anybody can see that he is my child. And after everything between us. He is mine!"

She continued to turn the stone over and over and then speaking slowly as one who teaches, she said, "You don't own nothing that I don't give you Nathan, *NOTHING!*"

Ownie watched him sensing his thoughts. If they were to come together, it was going to be now.

Nathan was remembering Martie's words. What did she say about women and life?

Suddenly, the woman beside him was speaking again. She said, "The child does need a father; my brothers don't live close any more. The child needs a father who will take care of him. You an' me, we did mean something to each other, Nathan, maybe we can raise the child together."

She sensed the emotion that raced through him, but he would not look at her.

Finally, with a sure gesture Ownie threw away the stone she held in her hand.

The action seemed to loosen the moment and release

both people, for turning to her with a faint trace of a smile beginning on his lips, he said, "So Ownie, maybe we name de child, Nathan."

Market Smarts

She got up early that morning, earlier than usual, because there was much to be done that day. Ned had already gathered all the bags of pimento and sweet potatoes and left them by the roadside. Before the sun rose much higher, the truck should be here. Miss Bess positioned her turban strategically on her head and reached for her purse.

She did not like to travel by truck, at least not in broad daylight; a bus would have been better, but what can one do?

Angie, her helper, was sick in bed, so she had to take the foodstuff into town. She had never done this before, but if Angie, who had hardly finished five years of elementary school and who was not known for her wit, could do it, certainly she, a school teacher learned in the English classics, could at least do as well.

Still, she felt just a little tense. She decided that she would not stand by the road because she could hear the whine of the truck from inside the house as it tackled

Spring Mount Hill.

She expected it soon, but who knows when it would come? Christened, *As You Like It* by the proud owner, the truck was known to stall on the road and not show up for hours. Bess remembered the brightly painted sign on the vehicle and thought: this is certainly a travesty on Shakespeare.

As she checked the contents of her purse, Bess wondered vaguely if she should have accompanied Angie at least once to the market.

She shrugged and dismissed the thought, for Angie would have known better than to have suggested that. After all, everyone knew Bess was Parson Hollings' daughter, and although he was dead, she still had to uphold the family name.

She did not belong in a market, squatting on a stool hollering out prices, haggling with higglers, and calling out to customers. No, she smiled ruefully, she did not belong there.

Already, on occasion, she had run into one of the up-and-coming young men in the local transportation business who was commonly known as *Lord Nelson*.

Intending to ingratiate himself with her, Nelson had bragged of the worthiness of his new bus that he called *Ever Ready*, and had stated with a good bit of suggestiveness that he favored her, and it was not only the bus that was ever ready.

Bess had dismissed the remarks as the words of a brazen man and had avoided him and others like him as much as possible. Yet, here she was, waiting for one of those reeling, rattling and unreliable trucks to take her to the market.

A knock on the door jarred her out of her musings, and she opened it to see Miss Mattie, her next door neighbor.

Miss Mattie had come to tell her that it was time she came out as the truck was liable to pass and not stop if nobody were outside by the bags.

Bess smiled and nodded. Mattie was right; she would go outside and stand and wait. Turning to check the room, she took her fan and followed Mattie to the gate.

There were four bags in all, not a lot by common standards, but enough. Miss Mattie, an entrepreneur, had retired from business only recently having given up her stall at Queen's Market in Montego Bay.

She had now become the designated advisor to the village on all business matters pertaining to merchandising, pricing and especially market demeanor. She and Angie talked and argued constantly over market affairs, but Miss Bess had never paid much attention to what was said. Now she wished she had.

Placing her hands on her hips, Mattie looked at the bags and turned to observe Bess.

Shaking her head, she said, "Miss Bess, Ma'am, I hates to interfere but you know, you look more like a school teacher than a sharp market woman. Dem people in town is sharp and so if you go lookin' like that, they are liable to think you don't know what you doin' and want the things you have for nothing.

"Now, where is your nice apron? Where is your broad straw hat and your nice sandal? Dem high heel shoes is just goin' to throw you down. I know you *are* a school teacher, but this is not the time to look like one."

Bess knew Mattie was right, but it was too late to change. She could hear the truck as it cried and belched its way up the hill.

Well, this will have to do, she thought. It can't be helped. The truck pulled up to a stop and the side-man hopped off and with Ned's help threw the bags over the high railing of the truck and perched them on top of other bags filled with produce.

That done, they turned to Miss Bess and with little ceremony hoisted her over the heads of passengers already seated and placed her into the third row.

The women here were seasoned veterans of market trucks and saw little that was unusual about Miss Bess' entry. Asking everyone to move or stand to allow her a more traditional entrance would have created disharmony. Now, they smiled her welcome and slid over graciously to offer her a place. When she had settled in, conversation already in progress simply continued.

Bess felt apprehensive.

The surroundings were more challenging than she had expected. She was overwhelmed by the cackle of chickens, the smell of turnips and fever grass and the endless chatter of her neighbors.

She tried to distance herself mentally, but was interrupted by a voice at her shoulder, "Pardon me. Miss Bess, you don't know me ma'am, but I used to know your father, Parson Hollings, when he was alive and my niece was in your Fifth Form class at school. I'm surprised to see you here, ma'am. Where is Angie?"

Upon hearing that Angie was sick, the voice continued, "This market-going business takes a lot of stomach and a strong heart. I hope you can stand up to it, ma'am."

Bess smiled and replied, "Thanks, but I think I can manage for if I understand Angie correctly, all I need to do is to take the bags to the market and wait for a Mr. Dan, the vendor to meet me. He will take the provisions and at the end of the day will give me the profits less his twenty-five percent."

"Well ma'am," the girl continued, "handling a man like Marse Dan is never easy. He is liable to tell you anything at the end of the day. I hear him tell people how bad business was and why he made so little while the money is in his pocket all the time. Do you know how much your foodstuff cost, ma'am? You gots to know that to figure up on Dan. You are a lady of learning, but market-going calls for smarts."

Bess thought over the advice carefully and thanked the young girl who said her name was Iris.

What she had said added to the pressure Bess was under, and slowly she could feel the muscle at the back of her neck beginning to tighten. She became decidedly nervous and apprehensive; her body felt hotter than before.

Already her stockings were sticking to her. Why did she wear stockings? She is not going to church; she is going to the market not to buy but to sell. She breathed a nervous sigh.

The sudden lurching of the truck, the stopping and starting every few minutes, was draining her energy. She could feel the sun on her head. Why hadn't she taken her hat? This was all going to be more trying than she had thought.

By the time the truck stopped in front of the large structure which was the market, Bess could hardly stand. Scores of vendors had flowed out of the building on to the streets and large crowds of people were milling about.

Hawkers were hawking their wares. Pushcart operators were darting in and out of the crowds.

School children in their brightly colored uniforms were busy buying sweets to take to school to save for recess.

Bess looked about her caught up in the swirl of the moment.

Suddenly, she remembered her bags. Fear flooded through her. How would she know which bags were hers? What were their markings?

After the truck was unloaded, the side-man pointed to four non-descript bags and said that they were hers.

By the time she walked over to them they were being looked over by two boys who asked solicitously if she needed help. Bess refused firmly and planted herself by the bags.

Pushcarts and handcarts were everywhere. Goods were being pushed in all directions. The sweet smell of peppered fried fish, *bammies* and cane sugar filled the morning air and drifted towards her.

She thought she heard Iris say to someone, "She is waiting for Dan."

Shortly afterwards, a pushcart operator arrived and said, "Ma'am, Dan send me. Dan send me, ma'am and him want you to follow me."

Relieved, Bess allowed the smiling, business-like fellow to stack the bags on the cart. He spun the cart around expertly, took off and shouted to her, "Follow me, ma'am follow me."

Bess started after him, frantically trying to keep up.

After a few minutes, he was nowhere in sight. He was swallowed up by the various colors, sizes, and shapes of people and things.

Miss Bess felt panic rising in her throat as she surveyed the throngs of people milling about her.

She wanted to cry out, but she couldn't.

All actions seemed to be happening in slow motion and the scene took on an eerie stillness, echoing the stillness within her soul.

Tears welled up in her eyes, and she neither saw nor heard the cries of the vendors as they called out to customers sauntering by.

Nor did she hear the laughing shouts of stout market women in their blue chambray aprons as they greeted each other. She did not see the men tottering on their feet as they crouched under the heavy load of large brown bags stuffed with provisions.

Standing on tiptoe, she peered over taller heads looking for the boy who had so expertly taken her bags. She looked, hoping that he would reappear when he realized that she was not with him.

Slowly she turned around and turned again until she almost fell over a bag of coconuts. What was she to do now? She looked vacantly into the faces in front of her.

One woman in a yellow bandana starched stiff and expertly tied, wearing a plaid dress and oozing Kush-Kush perfume, smiled at her sweetly and said in a cooing voice, "You looking for some nice breadfruit, Missus, or a tidy bag of *cho-cho* or mangoes? Some fresh mint, thyme or jelly coconuts, perhaps?"

Better go back to the truck, Bess thought, and she began to move through the crowd toward the entrance.

As she approached, Iris saw her and ran to her shouting: "Where you gone to, Miss Bess? Where you gone to? Marse Dan was just here lookin' everywhere for you and for the provisions."

Miss Bess looked behind Iris and saw Dan standing there, chewing a slim strip of sugar-cane stalk, one hand in his pocket as he leaned against the iron grating that marked off the perimeter of the market.

He smiled and began to walk slowly toward her. She heard him say, "Good morning, Miss Bess. What happened to the foodstuff ma'am? Me was looking for you all over de place."

Bess looked at him and suddenly she knew. She, Bess Hollings, had been robbed. Those bags of provisions were gone.

How was she going to tell Angie that she had come home with nothing?

What would Miss Mattie say?

Bess brushed the knuckles of her fingers slowly against her lips.

What was she to do with her grocery list?

Yes, she had been out-smarted. But she had learned. Maybe next time Angie comes to Market, she should talk with her about raising the profit margin with Dan to about eighty percent. After all, there is a lot of risk involved in this business.

Iris smiled regretfully and still trying to be helpful, said, "Yes ma'am, I understand ma'am. There is the *Ever Ready* bus right over there. Why don't you take it?"

Clutching her purse closer, Miss Bess turned to Iris and said, "Iris, you know every day no Christmas. I'm going to the police station and then I am going home, this time on the bus."

Clara's Move

Clara walked out of the house and closed the door gently behind her. Gently, because this was the way she was closing this chapter of her life. She took a few steps across the veranda and looked out at the garden. The ground seemed sparse, the plants stunted. It was a cloudy day. The sun had hidden itself since morning. Already it was mid-day and only a few rays were peeping through.

Bleak days are good too, Clara thought, as she took the suitcase which had been placed by the veranda gate earlier.

A day like today makes us think about how we feel inside, she thought.

Turning back, she gave the house one last look. The windows seemed shadowed. An eerie quiet had settled over the place. She had sold off most of the furniture after having given the best pieces to friends. The rest she had sent ahead by truck to the old family home, now her brother's residence.

The house had been brightly painted inside and out. The blue shutters with their orange triangular designs on spaced panels contrasted well with the creamy yellow of the walls. Yes, she had always liked bright colors and she'd never denied herself. She glanced at her neighbor's house painted only one color and found it drab in comparison.

Clara looked about at the yard one more time.

More could have been done with it, but she was so busy with making sense of all that had happened in her life and she was always so occupied with the clinic that little time was left for anything else.

Natty, the boy she had hired, had not been reliable. He had not watered enough. She should have let him go but she kept him on. He was his family's sole bread-winner.

But it was not the yard she had loved, it was the house. She had loved it as though it were a child.

She remembered walking through the front-door four days after her marriage to Jonas. They had just returned from her parental family-house where the marriage had been celebrated.

She recalled not the joy but the anxiety, the fear of failure that she carried with her. She had wanted so much to make a home for her new husband about whom she knew so little.

She brightened when she recalled the crisp curtains, the mahogany furniture, the embroidered table cloths, the crisply starched shirts, and the smell of cooked food and the general charm of the place.

She took a few more steps along the path toward the gate ... images of those early days of home-making drifted into her mind.

Suddenly, she looked up and saw a figure approaching her. It was Naomi Thompson, her neighbor.

"Good morning, Clara," she said. "It seems like de sun don't want to shine today."

Naomi, a stout and shapely woman, walked towards her from across the road with the slow undulating walk of a Caribbean woman who had seen it all, been through it all, had survived, and expected the cycle to start again.

She saw no reason to hurry. There was no challenge in life she could not imagine meeting or at least living through.

Naomi leaned against the gate, looked at Clara's suitcase and said, "So, the time has really come. You're leaving the old district. Lord, who goin' to help the mothers and the children? So, you goin' to live with Corey. Can't say that I blame you. This place must hold painful memories for you. We have to move on."

With resignation masking her concern, Naomi picked a bud from a nearby rose bush and handed it to Clara.

Unmindful of the prickles, Clara reached for it and, as was often the case, it pricked her finger.

Naomi stood helplessly and watched as Clara sucked the blood from the tiny wound.

"You can always come back to us,"

Naomi continued and then added a practical suggestion, "You could always get a smaller and different house."

Clara embraced her, cleared her throat and murmured, "Life is over here for me. I don't want to go, Naomi. I don't want to but I have to. With Jonas dead, I can't keep up the place. I need to make a new start. And as you know, the government is opening up its own health clinic. People will get help."

The two women had discussed all of this before. The silence between them now was warm and friendly but filled with quiet anxiety.

Clara released herself from the moment by remembering that she had to catch the bus to Johns Hall.

She picked up her suitcase again and started off down the road at a quick hustle turning her head to say, "The world no level, Sister Naomi; I will send word."

Clara established a brisk pace walking towards the cross roads, nodding, smiling and stopping to have a few words with those she met.

So many were the goodbyes that she got to the square only a few minutes before the bus arrived.

Safely seated in the vehicle, Clara began to reflect on her life. She couldn't really decipher the riddle of what had happened to her.

Was she leaving the life she knew or was it that the life she knew had left her?

She had married Jonas Nelson right after nurse's training and had gone to live with him in Kensington. He had been what her family called "a stable and good provider." And this was important in an uncertain world.

A hard working, good humored and religious man, he had divided his time between working the land, church duties, and playing dominoes in the late afternoon around a table in the square with friends. Never one to go far from home, he took care of all that he felt belonged to him.

She had accepted her marriage for what it was, and although at times she felt that there should be more, something more for her in this life, she was glad for what she had.

Clara had been raised to be grateful for the gifts that came her way.

Everyone knew that Jonas was a good husband. He was kind to her family in every way. Her parents thanked her for bringing such a man into the family.

She had smiled and gently reminded them that they had introduced her to him and had actively encouraged the relationship.

Jonas worked hard, complained little. He had loved her deeply and helped her in whatever way he could.

When she asked him to aid her in opening the health clinic for pregnant women and those with simple ailments for which she could provide remedy, he assisted and did not oppose her.

Clara was glad for something to do after the deep sense of loss following the still-birth of their son.

As a nurse, she kept herself busy birthing other people's children and dealing with mumps and measles outbreaks.

She was still young, in her early thirties, both she and Jonas felt that there would be time for children.

No need to panic. But it was not to be. Jonas up and died, just like that.

A robust, vigorous man ... never sick a day in his life.

Clara was shocked and deeply grieved by the turn of events.

Heart defect. Defective valve, the doctor had said.

Clara did not know until later when it was revealed to her that this defect had also killed his father.

She wondered whether her parents had known. After all, Jamaica is such a small place.

Clara was not like Naomi, who was open and receptive, free to dance on her porch or in the street, taking the world as it came, understanding intuitively the rhythm and pace of the life that flowed around her.

Clara was more internal ... more private, more difficult to read, as Jonas told her repeatedly. It was as though she had cordoned off a part of life and lived within its perimeters. Her world, like that of so many in her social class, was narrowly prescribed.

Deviation was frowned upon. Clara was raised to honor the timeless traditions and customs endorsed by family and upheld by Caribbean society. She knew the rules.

Clara had been close to members of the family on both sides and had been called on time and again to help out in several ways especially with loans and financial gifts.

After Jonas' death, she had thought of going to live near some of his relatives in Montego Bay but had decided against it as the pressures there would be more than she could bear.

Clara knew that she would eventually get her own place.

The bus hit a particularly nasty stretch of road at Sanguinetti and Clara found herself bouncing up and down on the hard seat. She had sold Jonas' old car. Now she wished she hadn't. She wished she had driven herself. Then she remembered that she had hoped to purchase an updated model as soon as she was comfortably situated.

Living with Corey would only be for a short time. A very short time. She needed to get on her feet and begin to rebuild her life.

The bus rattled on through miles of banana and breadfruit trees, stopping every now and then to drop off or pick up passengers.

Clara focused little on what was going on around her. Glancing out of the window, she noticed that the clouds had gone and the golden yellow rays of the afternoon sun were shining through.

The vivid colors of the Caribbean announced themselves: the sharp green of the leaves, the tinted blue of the distant hills, the bright intensity of the multicolored houses and the crowds of school children in blue skirts and white blouses, brown and beige, maroon red and pink, green and white uniforms with their straw hats held by ribbons laying on their shoulders, hugged the side of the road.

Their laughter and playfulness echoed in the air.

As the bus began its ascent into the mountains, Clara

knew that she was close to her destination and looked forward to arrival.

She silenced any concerns that still gnawed at her mind and returned her attention to the present. She got out of the bus in the town square feeling jostled and tired but buoyed by an eagerness to see her brother and to return with him to the family home. Corey, still unmarried, had remained in the house to take care of the family holdings and to add to it by his business ingenuity.

Smoothing out her dress, Clara picked up her case and started to walk towards the imposing looking shop where so many other people seemed headed. Corey had told her to wait for him there.

Passersby looked at her with interest and curiosity as she crossed the square, for she was a good-looking woman, well dressed in fine clothes, which, although showing signs of travel, also indicated some expense.

Only old Marianna Livingston, the retired school librarian, out for an evening's stroll, recognized her and stopped to greet her and to welcome her home. Clara recognized no one else and kept her focus on getting to the shop.

She didn't recognize the shop owner, but as she entered, he looked at her, smiled and said, "You are waiting for somebody, Missus?" "Yes," she said, "I'm waiting for Corey Hawkins. I am his sister, Clara from May Pen in Clarendon."

At this, the shopkeeper, a slim sinewy built brown-skinned man, who looked as though he had been an athlete in the past, began a smile which turned into a laugh.

"So you are she. I know you would be comin,' but I wasn't expectin' … I wasn't expectin' a nice woman like you. Corey talk much about you. So you're the younger sister!"

"Yes," Clara said attempting a smile to hide the fact that she was overwhelmed by the direct scrutiny of his attention, "I am the last one."

"Well, Corey and me, we do good business together, "the merchant chuckled and continued, "You want something to drink?"

He reached for and opened a cold bottle of tropical soda before she could respond, and poured it bubbling into a glass. Clara took it gratefully for she was thirsty.

She still did not get his name.

After taking a sip, she said carefully, "And you are?"

The man moved out from behind the counter and offered her a chair.

"I am Stanley Delaney. The Delaneys are not from these parts. We are really from Tangle River but we bought property 'round here because it is so close to Montego Bay and business is looking up. I hope that Corey mentioned me to you and said only good things …"

He laughed at his attempt at an ironic remark and continued, "Everybody call me Manny."

Clara was torn between standing and listening to the shop-keeper's comments or sitting in the proffered chair which did not look any too strong, considering that she was not a meager woman."

Manny read her mind and nodded to her, holding the chair firmly in place. Clara hesitated but finally sat down.

The merchant smiled at her reassuringly.

Clara had not heard of Manny or of his family before but hesitated to say so. Instead, she inclined her head so as to give the sign of agreement to whatever was being said.

Customers continued to file into the shop and Manny excused himself to slip back behind the counter to help his assistants in the cutting, wrapping and general transfer of goods; the money paid disappearing silently into the till under the counter.

As the shop emptied again, the merchant dusted off his hands and came around to rejoin Clara.

Sensing her unease, he said, "Don't worry Miss Clara, Corey will soon come. Now, Corey and me, we are good friends. We hit it off straight away and he helped me get situated in the district. We have other business ventures in the area and we're partners on a couple projects. I don't know if him tell you about them."

Clara shook her head and wondered why this man thought that Corey would discuss his business arrangements with her?

Corey and Clara's conversation centered only on family issues.

"Maybe, I could take your suitcase and you could sit in the room in back where you would be more comfortable," Manny said pointing to the back of the store where she would be away from the customers.

Clara smiled politely and declined.

"Don't trouble yourself. I know Corey will come soon. But thank you all the same."

Not to be outdone, and eager to please, Manny continued the conversation by explaining how he had improved the shop since he first bought it.

He had increased the stock and expanded the building with money earned from the neighboring plantation he had bought. Further, he had even built himself a nice house a little ways out of the center of the district but very accessible.

Clara tried to look interested but was becoming increasingly concerned about the whereabouts of her brother.

Then she heard the sound of a truck pulling up and heard Manny say, "Here come Corey now. I can tell the snarl of that old truck. We always have a drink together before lockup time."

Corey, a stout man who struggled against being overweight, walked into the store. He slapped Manny on the shoulder in a jovial and fraternal way and embraced then his sister, Clara.

"I am so sorry to keep you waiting, but the truck was giving me trouble."

"I'm glad to see you Clara. I'm so glad that you decided

to take my advice and come back home. At least for a while. I hope that Delaney here welcome you proper."

Clara voiced her agreement and began to reach for her suitcase.

Manny jumped up to get it for her, and grinning broadly at Corey said, "Miss Clara and me get along. We get along alright."

He stored the case in the truck and walked back to the door of his building, waving to them as they drove away.

Clara was happy to see Corey.

As her older brother, he was a symbol of stability and comfort to her.

She told him of the difficulties she had with the house since Jonas' passing and the regrets she had having to part with it.

She told him of the friends she had left behind, the memories and the closing of the clinic. She told him of the way she dealt with several of the emotional changes that threatened to overwhelm her.

Corey encouraged her to release all of these residuals from her mind and to start afresh.

He shared with her, something he had kept to himself, the cost involved with medical care for the old people at the end.

He had not bothered to trouble her with the bills, he said, since he had decided to take charge of the property. He did admit, however, that he knew that Jonas would always contribute, if called upon.

Corey followed up with questions regarding the disposal of her household goods and reiterated to her that the truck with the items she had elected to keep had arrived safely.

By the time they reached the house, Clara felt pangs of hunger moving in her stomach.

The smell of mutton stew, rice and peas and garden vegetables, all well laced with thyme and hot scotch bonnet peppers, rose to meet her as soon as she stepped out of the truck and entered the house. Clara laughed under her breath at the familiar smells, and began to feel relieved and almost happy.

She turned to Corey and said, "So, Marie still cooking for you?"

"I couldn't do without her," her brother answered.

"As you know, she stayed on after the old people passed."

Corey allowed Clara to enter the home before him and followed quickly with her suitcase which he thought to deposit in her former room.

Before reaching the bedroom door, he looked back at her and said, "Clara, I hope that you will like the changes that I made and be comfortable here."

Clara nodded and hurried into the kitchen to greet Marie, and to tell her how starved she was for her cooking. Marie accepted gratefully the only compliment she ever cared to receive, which was praise extolling her mastery of the local culinary arts.

She, in turn, told Clara how handsome and well she looked in spite of everything, and that she was most heartily welcomed home.

After the evening meal, Clara helped with the washing up before retiring to her room.

After a quick shower, not even the loud chirping of the chorus of crickets outside her window could keep her awake. She fell asleep as soon as her head hit the pillow.

In the morning she was awakened by the familiar full-throated voice of the neighbor's rooster and, after an additional snooze, by the cackling of the hens in the yard.

Breakfast was a grand affair. Marie outdid herself: codfish and ackee, roast dumplings, liver with onions, fried plantains, buttered hard dough bread, and Blue Mountain coffee. Who could ask for anything more? Not Clara.

Corey had stayed behind to have breakfast with her even though she had slept in and quite late too. She took note of his consideration and thanked her brother for his thoughtfulness. He brushed her remark aside by saying that this was the least that he could do after being so late to pick her up last night.

Clara smiled her appreciation, picked up her cup of coffee, and walked out to see the yard in broad day light.

Corey followed her. She complimented him on the changes: flourishing green shrubbery, blooming flowers, cut lawn, painted fences; nothing like the dry neglected ground she had left behind her.

If her yard looked like this, she wouldn't have to worry

about how much the impending sale would bring.

After she had taken the last sip of her coffee, Corey took the cup and said, "Before you woke, I drove over to Manny to talk about some business I had with him and lo and behold it was as though you had cast a spell on the man. He could talk of nothing else but you. Now, he's angry that I had not told him more about you and he worried about the impression he might have made on you."

Clara was silent, her eyes fixed on the yard. Corey continued, "I can tell you that he has taken a real strong liking to you, sister. I must tell you also that him and me, we get along well and do a lot of business together."

Then he laughed and said as though to himself, "We like brothers, man. In fact, I owe him money. Things round here not as good as it used to be. The Delaneys, they're well situated ... a finger in every pie, you might say.

You wouldn't be doing too bad yourself and you would help me if you could show a little interest in him. His wife passed a couple years ago. A nice man to have in the family."

Corey had said his piece and waited for his sister's response.

He wanted to alert her to the situation and thought it only right to give her time to think and to appreciate the opportunity.

Clara knew the importance of family.

As she listened to him, a calm settled within her and she remembered how strongly her brother had pressed her to come to stay and how eagerly he had anticipated her coming.

He had argued against her applying for a position at one of the big government hospitals in the city when she had mentioned it.

Clara had not forgotten how pragmatic he was either. A risk-taker, if need be.

Is this why he so eagerly awaited her coming and then was so late in picking her up?

Had he taken a risk on her?

She drew in a deep breath as the thought came to her. Who else had taken a risk on her? Had her parents also taken a risk on her?

Not looking at Corey, and showing little inclination to respond right away, Clara walked slowly to the end of the veranda for another view of the yard.

This time she looked out at the neighbor's posse of hens, chickens and the loud-mouthed rooster milling around together. They were feeding and were surprisingly quiet.

She surveyed the scene for a moment and then turning to face her brother, smiled ruefully, and said in a controlled voice devoid of emotion but clear and unmistakable in its conviction, "Coming home does not mean returning to childhood, Corey. I have grown and I have changed. I owe the family no obligation. Your plans with Stanley Delaney are your own. No offer that includes me is on the table.

"I love you, my brother, and I hope that all goes well for you in your business dealings, but know that *I claim my freedom.* I will not be bartered off. I will decide what I want. This is Clara's move!"

The House

The house was cool as Mrs. G. entered. The scent of fresh thyme drifted in from the garden under the window. The day was hot. She wasn't sure why she had decided to go to the market today. It could have waited 'til tomorrow. But one has to be business-like, Mama Lynn used to say. Well, she had tried; but what had it brought her? She felt hot and tired.

The coolness and silence of the house acted like a calming agent. She felt like resting on her bed, but going to bed in the middle of the day was weakness. Why should she take to bed if she wasn't sick? And she wasn't sick. She would indulge herself by sitting for a while.

She walked out to the veranda and looked out over the gully. The land was thick with foliage. It was almost mango season. The branches of the trees hung heavy with the small green unripe fruit. When last had she made mango jam? She couldn't remember. My God, so much has slipped. She sighed heavily, easing herself onto the wooden slated bench. The house and the land were all she had left.

She began to fan herself slowly, humming under her breath, *"Rock of Ages cleft for me. Let me hide myself in thee."* Church hymns always helped her feel settled.

So what is today going to bring her?

She wasn't sure whether she started to doze, but suddenly she thought she saw Dan coming up from the gully carrying a bunch of bananas. She could see the droplets of water on his rich dark skin. The damp shirt clung to his body. Something about the man always drew a response from her.

He waved to her and laughed. Putting the bananas on the step, he said, "I just come, Mrs. G. The fellows and I made about twenty yam hills today. A glass of cool river-water is all I need. You can't beat Hampton water for cooling thirst."

She would call Edith to bring it to him, making sure the girl took the water from the cool clay jar she kept in the pantry. The water shimmered in the glass on the small white embroidered linen cloth Edith placed in the saucer.

Mr. Gardner was a man who liked things done right. She knew it and respected him for it.

He noticed little things and she had always been careful to see to it that the niceties were kept to.

Mama Lynn was a woman who saw things the same way.

Fresh bougainvillea had to be placed in the house every day along with hibiscus if they were in bloom. Fresh spring water in the clay jars. Lemonade in the refrigerator and fresh hard dough bread and fruit jellies in the cupboard. Hot patties could be had from the local store.

She sighed. Following Mama Lynn's dictates, yes, she

kept house well for this man.

But look now where was he?

Was it six months or seven since the church had gathered to bury him? She would always tell him he was working too hard, but he wouldn't listen to her.

"Work is the lot of man," he would always say to her with his broad grin.

She felt the tears welling up in her eyes ... felt them splash on her hands folded quietly in her lap.

Quickly, she gathered herself together saying quietly, "No more of that. What would Mama Lynn say?"

She smiled to herself, raised up from the bench and called out, "Edith, Edith for God sake, where are you girl? Don't you know I come? Don't tell me you sleeping again. What you do since I gone?

We have coconut oil to make, you know. You grate the coconut yet? And what about the clothes? You hang them out? Koo-ya gal, its half a-day and you gone to sleep. Edith, I won't put up with it."

Edith ran out of the kitchen looking nervous and flustered. She knew Mrs. G. when she was like this. They had been together a long time. She knew how Mrs. G. carried on when she was worried and had things on her mind. And today she had things on her mind.

Who is going to work the land for her now that Mr. G. was gone? Will she be leaving the island to live with Samson? Edith knew all this, but she also knew better than to show it.

Squeezing the corner of her apron, she said softly, "Don't hassle yourself, Mrs. G. I picked some lemons this morning and made a nice pitcher of lemonade, ma'am. I will bring you a cool glass."

But Mrs. G. was not to be put off. She wanted to make sure all was in order.

She took her own apron from the rack and together with Edith she cooked the white flakes of the coconut until the golden oil swam on top. Then she took the pieces of grouper fish she had bought in town and fried them.

Old habits die hard, she thought, Mr. G. always liked a bit of fish on a Friday.

Exhausted from her efforts, Mrs. G. sat on the kitchen stool and looked out over the valley while Edith washed up.

What was she to do? Could she leave here and start over with Samson in a strange land?

She had visited her son some years ago, after Mr. G. had refused to go. She hadn't liked Miami. The noise, the hurry, nobody to talk to … cooped up all day in an apartment.

She left the kitchen and walked out into the yard. It had been newly sprinkled and swept.

So at least Edith had done something.

She wandered over to the herb and vegetable garden. It was just as Mr. G. had left it. The strong spicy smells drifted toward her.

Mint, which was so good for health, was growing in

green clumps. She stood for a while admiring the thick heads of cabbage. The cucumbers had done well this year.

Maybe with the pepper and the cho-cho she could make a good batch of hot pickles. Her garden had always brought her extra money, for everyone in the valley knew who made the best hot sauce.

Frustrated with herself for hugging the past to her, she left the yard and walked up to the gravel covered road.

The sun had cast a shadow which gave her shade. There was little traffic during the day, but right now there was none. The market trucks hadn't started to whine their way back as yet.

Folding her hands behind her back as was her custom, she thought: Look, Mama Lynn, what should I do now?

She felt her skin become moist with perspiration. All was quiet except for the clapping of her slippers on the stones.

Suddenly, she heard the sound of a dog barking. She heard the animal before she could make out its master. The dog was running ahead criss-crossing the road sniffing the bushes.

Mrs. G. placed her hands over her eyes to see if she knew the master. He approached her walking briskly, his machete hanging by his side. She could see from the dust that he had been on the road long.

She turned away to return to the cool of the house.

She hadn't reached the steps before she heard a voice say, "Good day, Mistress, my name is Sam, ma'am. I am related to the Thompson family at Spring Mount. I'm looking for day's work."

She was about to say she had nothing, when she caught herself.

She thought of the yams still in the ground, the bananas beginning to ripen on the trees and she heard herself say, "Edith, bring a cool glass of water for the gentleman."

Then turning to the stranger, she added, "Yes, I got day's work."

Remembrance

Mavis looked over the railings of her house on to the street below. She was wearing a light blue cotton house dress with white trim at the waist and round large front pockets. She felt comfortable and cool. The responsibilities and duties of the day were falling away and all was quiet except for the dull hum of vehicles passing by.

She planned to have a light supper and retire early. She had been attending to the workmen all day who were repairing the roof of the house damaged in the last hurricane. All had gone well and she was pleased with the results.

She looked down the length of her flower-lined terrace and her eyes caught the beautiful flower pot her cousin, Vera, had given her at the end of her last visit a couple of months ago. The terra cotta pot with its floral design stood out among the older grey planters.

Yes, Vera had been a good house guest. Full of conversation, there was never a dull moment with her.

Yet, she knew when to be quiet. She knew when to take

time alone reading novels she brought with her or the daily newspapers.

Mavis smiled in satisfaction for she liked Vera's way. She did not get into anything that did not concern her. She was not curious and made no attempt, under cover of being helpful, to search through boxes, drawers and trunks to make discoveries.

In fact, she made every effort to fit into the flow of the household and at times even offered to help her cook, Caro, in the kitchen to show off her skills.

Mavis sighed as images of her cousin cooking ackee and codfish with much too much coconut oil and too much scotch bonnet peppers came rushing back to her.

Caro assisted with the mincing of the spices but could do nothing but stand by and watch in astonishment as the preparation of the meal progressed. Everything was in excess. Caro always predicted disaster but somehow Vera would manage to pull it off.

Mavis entertained guests frequently but Vera was a favorite.

While other visiting relatives and friends used her home only as a base for their daily exploration of the island, Vera spent quality time with her and was a good companion.

They had a great times together reminiscing about the good old days and shooting the breeze while sitting on the terrace.

The focus of their conversation was on family issues, mainly, by way of inheritance dramas as the older ones passed away, local and international socio-political developments and, of course, local gossip.

Mavis was an avid reader. Her sight was not as good as it once was but still she read widely. Political journals, sent to her by relatives, and the local papers was her favorite material.

Sometimes she read historical texts if they were not too complicated and would peruse maps to remind herself of the capitals and cities of nations.

Vera, an attractive, charming and gregarious woman, read romantic and espionage novels and enjoyed the company of a range of friends and acquaintances, especially men, but always on her own terms.

She liked her freedom and although she was solidly middle class in her general demeanor and values, she held on to the independence and freedom maintained by the peasant class of women on the island who maintained their sexual freedoms.

It was generally known in higher social circles that some of these women took time to decide on the father of their children.

Middle class men who were surprised at being named by their peasant consorts were commonly said to have been given a "*jacket.*"

Vera, given her place in society, would not dare to think of taking such liberties for she would become a social outcast. Yet, she chaffed at the rules that confined women and in her own way, pressed at the boundaries.

She loved living abroad, but wanted the best of both worlds. Since her divorce, she returned to the island frequently to enjoy herself, spending time with friends and relatives when she decided such pleasurable visits were warranted.

More than a decade younger, Vera was more flexible, easy-going and had a great sense of humor. She took life as it came and did not ask for much. A free-spirit, she had married while overseas and had enjoyed several love affairs after the dissolution of that ill-fated union.

She was not a member of any particular religious denomination and declared that she went to church for the music and the sense of community.

Mavis, the older relative, managed a well-organized household and was strict and disciplined in her ways. She was a private woman who did not discuss her affairs with outsiders. Even family members were carefully selected if they were to be confidants.

As a strong supporter of her church, she was generous with her gifts. She recently gave her piano to the parish when she decided that it was not getting enough use in her home. Yet, she attended service only when so inclined, even though the minister visited her frequently to give thanks for donations.

Mavis and Vera enjoyed a strong relationship, bolstered probably by their differences. To Mavis, Vera was a breath of fresh air. She enjoyed hearing of Vera's escapades.

When on the island, Vera enjoyed the company of her old beau, Vincent Hodges, a man she used to know years earlier when she was a young girl and who was now a widower.

They would often go to the beach together, go out to dinner and sometimes Vera would return home very early in the morning being careful not to awaken Mavis. She was always happy and chirpy in the mornings telling Mavis of the clubs they had visited and the new delicious dishes she had tried.

At breakfast one morning, Vera remarked that she should have married Vincent when she was younger.

Mavis agreed with her and added, "Girl, it's not too late. Why not marry him now and come back to the island to live. Nice property selling up in the hills."

Vera smiled, poured herself another cup of coffee but made no response.

The sharp blast of a truck's horn roused Mavis from her reverie and she heard doors slamming in the building and voices calling out good evening to others. She knew that some of her tenants were returning from work.

Mavis thought it best to busy herself by doing something worthwhile to take her mind off the past and decided to get the basket with the peas out of the kitchen and shed them for tomorrow's dinner. Her brother would be in town and he would be joining her for the evening meal.

The repetitive motion involved in shedding the peas placed her in a meditative frame of mind. Mavis made a valiant attempt to shake off the nostalgic feelings that were encroaching and threatening to overtake her. She tried to hum a favorite song, but to no avail.

The flashbacks became more intense.

She wanted to stop thinking of Vera and her activities. But it was as though her cousin's *shade* had entered the house, as the old people used to say, and had made itself at home. There was no letting go.

Mavis had hardly made any headway in the shedding of the peas before Caro came to offer help and took the basket away from her. Her cook liked to be in charge of her kitchen and did not want any interference.

Mavis, now at loose ends, was thrown back into a reflective state of mind.

Seated on one of the softly cushioned terrace chairs, her thoughts quickly returned to the past and she entered a state of peaceful reverie.

Floating about in her head were memories of her own life as a young woman ... a woman much younger than Vera. She thought that the door to these memories had been closed a long time ago.

But, these images, accompanied by intense feelings of loss and longing were getting stronger. She tried to fight these encroachments but finding it futile, she decided to let go, give up resistance and follow her feelings and her thoughts.

Mavis recalled the day she first met Percy Mitchell, her former husband. His long, narrow face and deep-set eyes now took shape in her consciousness.

This surprised her for she had not thought of him in some time. Yet, here he was. Then, she saw her own face:

oval-shaped, dark-skinned, high check-bones, with a happy gap-toothed smile.

As a young woman, she was very enterprising and had gathered sufficient funds to purchase a retail store with a small rum shop attached which she managed while living on the floor above it.

Mavis liked being a business woman and her shop was a success. She enjoyed the interaction with her customers and they spent money with her.

She first met Percy when he entered the shop with a group of men who were her customers and good friends.

After the introduction, she had poured them *rum punches*, rum mixed with fresh tropical fruits, *house of lords*, strong white rum, cold milk with a touch of sugar and cool lemonade to refresh them on such a hot day.

The men relished the cooling drinks, conversation and laugher filled the air and they thanked her profusely. She was kept busy preparing food for those who were hungry and seeing to their general comfort.

These customers had standing in the community. Several worked for important commercial businesses in town such as the local banking establishments, legal offices or were members of the city council.

She had known many of them for years and knew that she could count on them for a favor or two should the need arise.

Percy was the new man in the group.

During a quiet moment when she queried one of her

friends to find out more about him, she found out that he was in the transport business and was visiting from the capital city.

This visitor, tall, light-skinned and good-looking was still an enigma to her. He laughed easily and had a great smile. He was a man's man, at ease in the company of other men.

Yet, there was something about him that piqued her interest. He did not approach her to make connections as others would considering that he might be returning to town in the future.

He kept his distance, yet he never took his eyes off her.

She felt his gaze.

At first she ignored him and then she looked back. Surprisingly, he looked away and appeared nervous and apprehensive.

Mavis laughed to herself for she knew that he sensed the questions in her straight-up gaze. She was very comfortable with men as friends but was not interested in relaxing amorous encounters.

Her eyes had asked, "What are you looking for ...? What are you interested in ...?

For all his keeping his distance, when the other men drove off, he stayed behind to speak with her and so began their friendship.

Mavis discovered that he was originally from the parish of St. Elizabeth, dabbled in real estate and was working on building a fleet of trucks to transport produce all over the island.

At present he had two trucks with one additional driver. He was a man with prospects.

Percy was clearly a man-of-the-world. Relationships with women were not unknown to him.

Yet, there was a charming little-boy quality about him that made him appealing to Mavis.

He trustingly shared his hopes and dreams with her and was able to laugh at himself in an amusing self-depreciating way that made her protective of him. Sensing his vulnerability, she saw where she could support him.

Slowly, she grew to care for him and to love him.

Whenever he was in town, they found time to travel into the country near Springfield where her family still owned a parcel of land and the family home.

They went there to be alone, to picnic and to have some time together.

They enjoyed each other's company. There were times she went with him in his truck on some of his longer in-land delivery trips.

She enjoyed the intimacy of sitting next to him as he drove, his long legs sometimes touching hers. She enjoyed his attempts to impress her by pointing out sites along the way with which he was familiar always accompanied by elaborate explanations.

Percy seemed to thrive in Mavis' company. He came to life and his goals and dreams appeared reachable and palpable.

He saw himself surmounting obstacles as he enlarged his sphere of influence. He felt that he could make plans and do things.

During their courtship, Percy showed the care-taking side of his nature by bringing along pillows to support Mavis on the longer hauls.

He made more frequent stops so that she could stretch her legs. At various points along the way, traveling through small villages, he called vendors to the side of the truck to bring her fresh fruits: star apples, mangoes, sweetsops; salt and pepper shrimps; jerk pork; escoveitched fish etc. and introduced her to new dishes such as turtle soups, pork chaw sow and calves feet jelly at his favorite cook-shops.

Mavis was welcomed by all his friends and proprietors on the road. Everyone know this was his lady.

Percy enjoyed Mavis' company because she was an open-hearted, loving and vital woman.

She loved good company, good food and was a great cook.

When she balked at trying dishes she had never had before on the road, he would say with a smile and much conviction: "Don't worry, Mave, all of this is good for you, make you put on a little weight."

Clearly, he favored plumb women even though he being as scrawny as he was never gained an ounce.

On these country drives, Mavis also shared her dreams with Percy. She told him of her desire to visit the United States and to spend time with her sister who worked in

New York City. She hoped not only to visit but to remain there to work for a couple of years and then return home to enlarge her shop and build a home.

Percy was supportive of her dreams and was eager to talk about what they could build together.

This new man in her life made a place for himself in Mavis' family. He had a pleasant way about him that put people at ease, and a smile that broke down all of Mavis' defenses.

Their friendship grew. They became lovers. Later, they were married.

It was a simple country wedding in the church Mavis had attended most of her life. The reception was small but festive. Friends and family were happy to see Mavis wed at last.

Some feared that she might become a spinster for she seemed totally uninterested in making any attempt to catch a good husband.

Mavis, for her part, independent, outgoing and enterprising had no such fears. She led an active and busy life with family and friends and prided herself on being a shrewd and successful business woman.

She saw the fragility of casual relationships based solely only on sexual attraction and was not inclined to go for a care-free romp in the sheets with any man for the thrill of it. She valued herself and she hoped for a partner, not only a husband.

Now, she was in love with this tender and loving man.

There was deep sexual attraction between them but they could make plans together as well. She thought him, her husband and her friend. They could make a life together. She felt that she had found the one she wanted. Mavis could be heard laughing and talking happily with her customers. Her deep mahogany skin shone with a rich inner radiance. Life was good.

The day came when Mavis' sister sent her an invitation to come to New York City and arrangements were made for her to make the trip. Percy and Mavis talked the matter over from every angle.

It was a brave step for Mavis to take but she was a woman with hopes and dreams for herself, her husband and her larger family. She was fearless, indeed, intrepid. She felt that others had made this journey abroad and so could she.

Mavis spent time reading about her destination. America appeared to be a dream-land where all things were possible.

This was her chance and she knew it. Many considered her fortunate and would have liked to be in her shoes.

In a short time, she obtained a work permit and left the island for New York City.

Everything was planned.

Percy would help her brother with the store and oversee the books while building his own trucking business. Their life together had been short but sweet. She was going to miss him, but this had to be done.

This step had to be taken if they were to have a chance of success in life.

But, Mavis did not find New York City to her liking. Hard work in the kitchens, house-keeping duties for rich whites or factory work were the only choices.

The pay was good compared to the island but the work was mind-numbing. She was not accustomed to this kind of life.

On the island, she had her own servants and more freedom.

Further, the winter was cold and brutal. The summer was hot and heavy. There was concrete everywhere, very little time off and no respite. There was no pleasure or enjoyment here for Mavis in this new world.

Her sister had joined a new religion from the Middle East that kept her busy and she spent time mainly with her fellow-travelers. Mavis showed little interest in joining the faith and so was left on her own.

She was lonely, even though she met working women and men from other islands who were largely in the same boat as she was.

Nothing deterred her.

She was determined to make her stay a success. After all, she and Percy had plans. She strengthened her resolve by calling to mind images of her former life in great detail and keeping the images of loved ones in her mind and heart.

She wrote home bi-weekly, saved money, spent as little as possible and lived for the day when she would return to the island.

Love for her husband and for her island was synonymous. It was the fuel that kept her going.

Percy kept her abreast of what was taking place.

He was not a good writer and so the letters were not as newsy as she would have liked, but he did hit the salient points and she was satisfied.

From time to time, he declared that he did not see how he could live or go on without her. In her response, she reminded him that she loved him and that she would be gone for only three years, the length of her contract. She encouraged him to keep his spirits high.

After a time, Percy's letters began to fall off and came less and less frequently. At first, Mavis thought that he was just too busy.

But other letters began to arrive from family and friends reporting that Percy had taken up with another woman or women.

The shop was falling apart. The transport business was in shambles.

Mavis was surprised for she had been sending money home from time to time to firm up their financial accounts.

At first, she did not give full credence to these reports.

She felt that these developments were temporary assignations … men being men. He was just fooling around.

She would just have to put a stop to it. She had every confidence that things would work out between them.

However, when she heard that Percy had moved into another woman's house and was living with her, Mavis packed her bags, left New York and returned to the island.

She did not see Percy during the first month of her return home.

Heart-broken, angry and shamed, Mavis wept and could not be comforted.

She came to know that Percy was living in the well-appointed home of a successful nurse up in the hill above the town.

Mavis sent several messages to him but Percy did not respond.

Three months passed and finally she was forced to face reality. Slowly, she gathered up the reins of her life in her hands and began to re-energize the business and to restructure her priorities.

First, she repainted the building that housed her shop and then she replenished the stock in her storeroom. She reconnected with friends and began to take part in the public life of the community.

Mavis heard the unspoken words of many whom she met: "Poor woman. Husband gone and left her for another woman. Dat foolish man. I wonder how she stand it? Maybe she should have stayed in de island rather than travel to foreign."

Mavis said nothing. She led the conversation elsewhere

when the topic came up. She held her head up and went about her business.

Time passed. Interest in the estrangement between she and Percy began to die down.

Then, new rumors spread through town.

Gossip and speculation began to spread. Dry laugher could be heard everywhere the subject was discussed.

There was trouble between Percy and the nurse.

The new woman suspected him of being unfaithful to her. Gossip-mongers were happy and the talk was salacious. Who was the *new, new* woman? What a state of affairs!!

The irony of the situation was not lost on the towns-people. Mavis smiled at the news and was heard to remark bitterly, "Poor woman. She should have chosen better."

As the break between Percy and his mistress became obvious to all, Mavis took the opportunity to send one more message to her husband.

She told him that she had a gift for him. A gift she had brought from New York but had not the opportunity to give to him. She asked him to meet with her at the store.

A day later, Percy appeared.

He was thinner, scrawnier than ever but there was a macho air of bravado about him. He formed his face into a smile and asked Mavis how she had been.

She offered him a thin smile back and said life was hard but she was making it.

She mixed him his favorite drink which he took and drank greedily.

She noticed how hard things were for him. His shoes were worn and broken and his clothes had seen better days.

Then smiling her most charming smile, Mavis took the forms given to her by her lawyer, laid them before him and said in her sweetest voice, "Percy, we had our chance and we didn't make it. Let us call it quits. The lawyer give me the divorce papers. Just sign here."

Percy shocked, grimaced and moved away.

He glanced at the newly stocked shop and said, "Why should I divorce you? I thought you call me to talk about getting back together. Who say we can't make it?"

Anger welled up in Mavis' throat but she kept calm.

This was her opportunity and she would not let it slip. "Percy," Mavis continued, "We had our chance. It's gone now, man. Let it go. No temper, man. Here is what I have for you. If you sign right here, you can go to the Watson's Motor Vehicle Dealership in town and select a brand new truck, all paid for."

There was silence … a pause. She saw the shock in his face, but he turned away and still refused. She did not rush him.

"I will give you time to think," Mavis said gently.

Percy pounded his fist on the counter and said never, never would he agree to such a deal.

Never would he sign the document. She was his wife

and would remain so.

Mavis said nothing for there was nothing to be said.

She knew that he was angry and ashamed for he had been a fool. This is the best deal he would ever get from her.

Deep down, he knew it.

Customers were coming into the store and she had to go to help her assistant at the counter.

She said to him before parting, "I will leave the papers at the lawyer's office. Just sign it and pick up your brand new truck whenever you want."

Percy searched for words to say to her but found none, for he had no counter proposal.

He stormed out.

Two days later, the lawyer told her that the papers had been signed and she was a free woman.

Mavis rejoiced, took her freedom and never looked back.

She returned to the United Sates and remained abroad for several years.

Later, she came home to build a beautiful home in town. In fact, she owned several homes which she used as rental property.

Percy's relationship with the nurse did not go well. He took up with yet another woman. He moved away and dropped out of sight.

People would tell Mavis that they had seen him here or there in several different places.

Years passed.

Gossip had it that he died and was buried in the capital city. Mavis made no enquiry and did not encourage those who felt it their duty to keep her informed.

Life went on.

When shopping in town, if Mavis encountered the nurse, she gave a pleasant and courteous nod and simply kept on walking. On-lookers were surprised and puzzled by her lack of animosity and her calm detachment.

But the ache inside was gone. The sorrow and the loss were gone as well, but when triggered, the memories of the past so finely etched in the spyche would come flooding back.

This afternoon was such a time.

She had to let the guard-gates down and allow the images, the conversations, the whole experience to flow through her consciousness unimpeded. If blocked, these feelings would overpower and overwhelm her.

With time, Mavis' understanding had deepened. In many ways, we are our experiences. She had felt the cold, bone chilling wind of life in her face. It had spun her around but it had not broken her.

She had not run away or denied the hurt
She had not buried it so deep that it was unreachable
She had not projected it out to others
She came home to herself.

At first there was *anger* and *rage*, then there was *sorrow* and *sorrow* became *forgiveness.*

Finally, Mavis admitted to herself with the grace that comes with age and distance that *Percy never knew her. He never really knew her. He wanted her. He married her but he never knew her.*

She wondered now if he knew himself. Did he know what needed healing within him?

She had taken him at face value not understanding the fears, the compulsions that drove him.

In a world where one is so afraid of losing, one is also afraid of winning.

Mavis had put regret aside. She had accepted the challenges as they came, and held no bitterness. She never married again. She had taken no lovers either.

Mavis had given her love to her family, especially, her nieces and nephews. She supported the education of several of these younger members and now was recognized as the matriarch of the family. She had lived alone but was never lonely.

The matriarch left the terrace and as she turned to enter her drawing room she noticed that the lights were coming on in Morris Park for another night of community festivities. Tonight, she thought it might be a football game. She enjoyed the game and had high hopes for the local team.

She picked up a collection of poems written by one of her relatives and read:

> *Be at peace with your decisions*
> *Decisions taken from the heart*
> *Decisions taken in the silence*
> *Decisions reached through inner prompting*
> *Decisions that bring peace to the soul*
>
> *Be at peace with your choices*
> *Your past, your future, whatever is to come*
> *Move forward in the center of your path*
> *Full of inner knowing.*

Suddenly, the phone rang and Mavis wondered, could it be Vera planning to come for another visit?

Annaise Returns

A hush settled over the camp that evening as the women hurried to find food for the whimpering children and for the men who sat speaking in low voices to each other, or staring off silently into the distance in shocked disbelief.

The destruction was so wide-spread that it seemed incomprehensible. There had been no time to think. No time to call out. No time to protect the loved ones. No time, even, for self-pity.

The shock was palpable, as was the air of disbelief. How could this have happened?

How could the solid earth give way and collapse so completely beneath them … revealing the abyss? Bearing the pain of this unbearable agony, many felt themselves more dead than alive.

Although numbed by grief, their unruly thoughts kept returning to ever encircle those who had gone so swiftly, and without warning.

The memory of the cries of the entrapped haunted the consciousness of the survivors. The voices of trapped children, the voices of dying adults calling out for help from beneath the rubble, the muffled unrecognizable sounds that emanated into the air from the bowels of the earth while parents, friends, family members, everyone screamed out in agony and pain as they dug with bloodied hands and with whatever tools they could find tearing open the now solid earth.

Many continued to scratch away at the ground, even when they knew all was lost and that it was too late, murmuring to themselves: "*Bon Dié, au secou! Bon Dié, gain pitié*" (*God help us! God, have mercy.*)

For days the awareness of many survivors swam in and out of consciousness.

The world had become nightmarish and surreal: the makeshift tents, the screams of the children, the silent weeping and the confusion of the wandering ones, the odious smells, the search for water, food and medicine, the search for lost family members, the search for light during the dark nights and the endless queries about the dead as their names were repeatedly called out during the day…

The faces of the living bore the ravaging marks of the tragedy. The mood was one of dire urgency in Port-au-Prince, Haiti, the decimated capital city.

But the call to life was strong and the women prepared whatever food could be found to feed the hungry.

The helpers and aid-workers from across the seas brought medical supplies and water to assuage the growing demand.

They worked to support life, to comfort and to strengthen the bonds of life. The need was greater than they had imagined, and resources were scant.

Then, late one night a swift current of air moved through the camps, and soundlessly an entity spun itself into being from the spiraling vortex of energy that had broken the time-space continuum.

The implosion of the earth, the shock of the departure of so many souls, the pain of those who hung between life and death and the misery of the living had charged earth's etheric field and thinned the veil between the dimensions.

The entering entity knew that this was the time to return to the earth-plane. It was time to return to this beloved land.

The people had endured the unendurable, the unthinkable, the unimaginable.

Again, as in times past, the well-spring of life must be found.

The people must come together, and women are especially gifted to lead the way in the rebuilding of the new community. They must be the catalyst.

They must show the way.

Slowly, the entity formed a female light-body about itself and moved into the tents.

There was music in the air, for in the darkest of times it is music that sustained her people.

The anchoring rhythms of the drum pounded its

stabbing beat into the earth while the haunting, melan-
choly tone of the mourning flute wove its melodic line in
the night air as the earth spun away from the sun.

The entity observed the musicians and heard the flute
player cough in his thirst as he pressed his instrument to
dry lips to release once again the plaintive tones that rose
from the emptiness in the depth of his being.

Behind him the gourd-player belched out deep guttural
groaning notes.

The camp heard the music without listening, for many
were in a deep trance having freed their spirits, allowing
them to spiral out, floating free from pain, on the vibra-
tional arc of the sound.

The unseen visitor moved between the thickly set tents.

No one seemed to sense her presence, no one except for
Yvette, who having put aside her cooking pots, stood erect
and still, her psychic net attuned to incoming stimuli.

The seer sensed a strange presence.

This slender woman, ever vigilant and alert, lifted her
head, closed her eyes and drew in a long, deep breath which
she then slowly released.

She knew that there was a visitor in their midst. Slowly
and quietly, she mouthed the questions: "Ki moun ki la?"
(*Who is here?*) "Ki moun ou ye?" (*Who are you?*)

The response came with great clarity: "*Cé Annaise!*" (I
am Annaise.) Yvette heard the name even though there was
no sound.

"But, what are you doing here, lady? Have you come to help us?" she asked urgently.

Yvette waited, a slight expectant tremor moving through her body. A great calm descended over the tents before the lady replied:

"When my people suffer, I am here.
When the children cry, I am here.
When the streams run dry, I am here.
When the stores are empty, I am here.

When the men no longer know what to do,
I am here!

Today …

Together, we must again find the river's head.
Together, we must again find the source.
Together, we must replenish the land.
Together, we must give the people hope.

As Manuel and I did in days long gone
When we showed the way…"

Yvette rung her hands together, held tight her stomach and muttered irritably, "Lady, these are kind words, but these are hard times. Such hard times! I have survived the worst of times but never this. Never this!"

Yvette continued:

"We live in a sepulcher. We are all in the tomb. Our loved ones are buried untimely beneath the earth, beneath the earth, lady. How can we who are left hold on to life?"

Annaise's answer came back falling upon her ears as gently flowing water on parched land:

"Woman, take the bitter with the sweet; Hold your center.
You carry the source within you,
The head-water of the life's river
The source is within you;
You are at the threshold ... Haiti Rises!!!
The long night is behind you; the bright day is ahead;
This land is making a passage to another place,
Another space ...
Those who held sway,
Whose punishing hand held sway,
Their power is broken, their time is at an end.
No more will they make the children cry, No more will they make the land bleed ...
    A sepulcher, a desert ...
No more will they gorge upon your flesh,
As they grow fat;
A new day is come ... I bring the news!!!
I know the source of the spring, the head-waters,

I know the secret place, the hidden flow.
Reach within yourself, recreate your world;
You are not alone; do not yield the truth;
Do not abandon and walk away,
    Show the way,
Tell the others to hold!

The Spirit proceeded to tell her a story:

On our own mythic journey, my beloved Manuel shared the discovery of the head-stream of the river with me.

It was there by the water that I lay in his arms and our child was conceived.

It was I who called a gathering of the women of the village to define for ourselves what needed to be done. We told the men the kind of future we wanted for ourselves and for our children.

It was us women who led the way and brought the warring clans together, sharing the water, replenishing our lands and rebuilding community.

The Spirit said:

Hold to your strength, firm and unyielding.
    your stride, long and steady,
Your heart loving and strong,
    your faith deep and abiding,
Your love rich and nourishing,
your kindness tender and healing,

Your generosity, a steady stream,
your divinity blessed and pure,
Your magnificence sure!"

The light dimmed and in a moment the entity was gone.

All was quiet.

Yvette looked off into the distance, wondering if she had had a dream or maybe seen a vision.

Who was this visitor who entered this place on this night and knew so much about this land and its people?

Yvette rolled the matter over in her mind, seeking explanations.

Who is this Annaise?

Yvette sensed both her anguish and her power.

Her strength and her commitment were palpable. That she knew and loved this land was without doubt.

The rich imagery that her language evoked, and the wisdom buried deep in her words led Yvette to envision a new future for herself and for her homeland.

Yvette decided that tomorrow she would share the substance of this *visitation* with her close friends Solange and Marianne. Both she and Marianne were *Guédés* and knew well the workings of the *Loas*. Together, they had participated in many communal ceremonies to heal the sick and clear passage for the dying.

Solange was not as attuned to the world of *vodun*, but she honored and respected its powers and its traditions.

She was a teacher who had spent many years in school and had learned many things.

Maybe she would know who this great messenger Annaise is. Most certainly, she would know of her and of her partner, Manuel.

Tomorrow, she would speak with Marianne and Solange.

But tonight, she knew one thing, and it was that she must call a meeting of the community of women. Yes, she would do it. She was sure of it.

The movement of the tiny fetus within her body roused her from her thoughts as she looked up at the clearing night sky.

Author's Note

Annaise, the dynamic heroine in Jacques Roumain's celebrated novel, Les Gouverneurs de la Rosée, (Masters of the Dew) led the women of her community to call for cooperative action or a *coumbite* to bring water from a spring discovered in the high mountain by her beloved Manuel to restore life and build community in their parched and drought-ridden land. This action restored life to the village allowing the men to set aside the fights and blood-feuds that had divided them for generations. One of the great couples in literature, Manuel and Annasie's heroic leadership brought healing to the community; albeit at a cost to themselves as Manuel is killed in the effort. To many, Annaise epitomizes the grace, strength and resourcefulness of the Haitian woman.

Calypso Justice

Mr. Harrisford James took his crisply starched shirt from the rack and gingerly began to separate the folds which were resolutely stuck together.

Well, he thought, Lizzie is a meticulous home-maker, but starching shirts is not one of her strengths. This thing is a battering-ram. He grimaced as he weighed the situation and wondered whether he should even bother trying to put it on. Maybe, another shirt, less intimidating, might yet be found in his closet.

One glance at the clock, however, told him that he should not only try to get into the shirt but accomplish the feat very quickly.

Time, which generally was of no consequence to Mr. J., was of the greatest importance today. He wanted to be early in the office to assume an air of authority and impress the Huggins family as to just how hard-working and meticulous a Justice of the Peace he was.

As the Justice buttoned the sleeve of his shirt, which by this time was refusing valiantly to be folded smoothly into the waist of his pants, his thoughts once again shifted to the problems of the Huggins family.

Why are these Huggins forever fighting, he asked himself. Since grandfather Huggins died less than a year ago, the clan had known little peace. The bone of contention, of course, was the land. How was it to be divided up and who was to profit or not, as the case might be, from the provisions grown there?

Now, Sammy, the eldest of old John Huggins' sons, a thin, raw-boned, contentious and cantankerous man by nature, was threatening to chop up his own son-in-law, Ned, a likeable enough lad, whose alliance with his daughter, he had opposed.

Threats repeatedly pointed to a fatal outcome, if this young man and anyone else from the second generation of the Huggins family were ever to set foot on the family land and take provisions from it without his expressed permission.

Sammy suspected or discovered that Ned had been taking coconuts, cutting and selling bananas from the property in the name of Winnie, Sammy's daughter and Ned's wife. Ned argued that he had a right to take Winnie's fair share of the produce and sell it to help their family.

Sammy disagreed and as his threats increased, an alarm was sounded by other family members calling for arbitration before there was bloodshed. And so, the case was brought before Harrisford James, Justice of the Peace, Parish of St. James.

Mr. James took his role very seriously and considered

himself to be the local authority on the settling of disputes.

And since the number of disputes referred to him seemed endless, he had considerable practice in sharpening his skills.

James considered himself learned and well-educated gentleman and a respected leader who, as a consequence of his lofty role, must maintain some distance from the masses.

From his position he dispensed advice and offered guidance to the community.

He made sure that complainants appreciated his erudition by employing convoluted sentences and by sprinkling his pronouncements liberally with polysyllabic words adorned by use of his favorite verb tense, the future pluperfect: *will have been or shall have been ... etc.*

This morning, Mr. J. will have need of his entire arsenal of rhetorical devices because the Huggins family is not easily impressed. This was going to be a difficult day, but even he did not realize just how difficult.

As he readied himself to walk out the door, Mr. J. wondered about Lizzie.

She had left a week ago to tend her mother who was recovering from an illness and she had not yet returned. During the interim he was forced to assign that rascal, Alvin, to help out with her duties. Alvin was good enough in the yard, but in the house he was useless.

All Alvin knew how to cook was soup. Cooking soup, to his mind, involved pouring hot water over whatever food he could find and leaving it to simmer until he remembered to turn off the stove, by which time no one knew what the ingredients were to start with.

Lizzie, now, there's a woman who knew how to cook—from jerk pork or chicken to curried goat to hot pepper pot soup to stew fish, fried plantains and sweet mango chutney. Lizzie could cook them all and sweet too.

But where was Lizzie? Mr. J. wondered with growing annoyance as he laced up his boots.

Picking up his briefcase and walking to his car, he noticed that Alvin had already spied his approach and had begun to work purposefully, clipping the rich, dark green foliage of the hedge while singing under his breath the most irreverent of the bawdy songs which could be heard on the local music charts.

Mazie raise up her sweet head from de pillow
Groaned an' said, Marse Tom, Oh Marse Tom,
I need something to put out de fire
I am feeling hot, hot, hot ... Oh! so hot ...
Wheee !!!

Laughingly, Alvin waved at his boss and called out a strong "Good morning."

Mr. J. threw his briefcase on the back seat of the car and considered whether he should reprimand the saucy boy because he found the words of the song disrespectful or ignore the whole matter and offer him a modest and temperate greeting instead. He opted for the latter.

"Good work, Alvin, man; shape them up nicely for me."

Alvin flashed a row of sparking white teeth and said good-naturedly, "You can count on me, Mr. J. You can count on me. Work no frighten me, you know. No, sir. I always do a good job for you, sir."

Mr. J. knew that Alvin took no pleasure in gainful employment, not when there were shade trees to be slept under in the heat of the mid-day sun and petty thievery to be engaged in.

He was familiar with the young man's mischief and knew that he had to be tightly managed.

Deciding not to appear overly impressed by Alvin's marginal performance and wishing to change the tenor of the conversation, Mr. J. said, "And by the way, tell Lizzie when she comes, for I think that she is coming back this morning, tell her to make a nice dinner tonight. Maybe red beans sauce over white rice and some jerk chicken. Tell her to pick some tomatoes and *cho-cho* and cook them with fresh *callalo* and plenty of red pepper. And don't forget the plantains. I might bring someone back for dinner."

Mr. J. paused reflectively for a moment and thought that list just might be enough. Alvin nodded agreeably and on seeing his acquiescence, Mr. J. started his car and drove away.

As the Justice negotiated his way through the traffic of the busy town square, the musicians and local performers were already out practicing their art in the park for performance later at the hotels and at the upcoming dance. Several were rehearsing, improvising and, in general, warming up their instruments.

Don't these people have anything better to do, thought Mr. James. They are a damn nuisance. Look at them just hanging about socializing, looking for enjoyment rather than real work.

I bet that they are living off the government. Mr. James wanted nothing to do with them unless they came before him in dispute.

It was as though the people in the square were aware of his feelings, for very few went out of their way to acknowledge his presence. No passing motorists blew car horns by way of a friendly salute and no one smiled and called out his name as token of friendship and esteem.

Walking quickly to the post office, an imposing building at the corner of the square, Mr. James required his mail of the postmistress and received a packet of envelopes which he placed securely in his briefcase. Within a few minutes, he was turning into the complex of buildings which housed the court house and the police station, ready to assume his role as the parish's Justice of the Peace.

Lizzie, the absent housekeeper, having missed the market bus, was walking back to Mr. J.'s residence, her travel bag hanging across her body.

The week she had spent with her mother had been demanding. Aunt Dor, as her mother was commonly called by the locals, was about fifty years old and not in the best of health. She was hardly able to work the patch of land for her provisions and Lizzie had now to be sending her food almost on a weekly basis.

Lizzie had kept from Mr. J. just how ill her mother was so as not to alert him to the assistance she was offering. She knew how Mr. J. felt about the burden of large families. He claims that he had never hired a woman whose entire family he had not ended up supporting in one way or another.

Lizzie had taken that statement as a warning and had kept her family business to herself.

Still, she was getting along very well with Mr. J., seeking to please him by preparing his favorite dishes, keeping the house meticulously and even helping him keep the books on the schedule and pay of the workers on the small plantation.

She made sure that all flowed smoothly for him. The salary was not exorbitant, but there were benefits. He wasn't home much and she could generally do whatever she pleased.

Lizzie smiled with satisfaction as she walked along, pausing to say a gracious good morning to Miss Hilda who sat cross-legged on a pile of freshly broken stones. "Morning, Miss Hilda," she said, "you start early ma'am. I see you have a good pile already."

Lizzie smiled and pointed to the pile of stones each piece cut with expert exactness from the mother rock. Miss Hilda had been doing this precision work for some years now and wasted not one motion as she took each stone and hitting it with mathematical exactness watched it splinter into fragmented facsimiles.

Hilda was employed by the Public Works Department to break the stones that would be used to repair the local roads. It was back-breaking work, dogged and unrelieved, but chatting with passersby eased the monotony and placed her in a position to know all that took place in the district.

She looked admiringly at Lizzie who was well-liked in the community. She was a fine looking young woman: slender with firm, bold breasts, well rounded hips and strong legs.

She had been a good student at the local school and could have gone further if support had been available. Several young men had shown interest in her, but she kept herself to herself.

"So you going back to Mr. J. now?"

Without waiting for an answer, Hilda changed the subject, "How is you dear mother, Dorothy?

I wonder if she take the chainey root tonic I boil for her? Marse John, my neighbor, swear by that drink, says that it works for man and beast alike. And I believe him too, for look at that man, never sick a day in his life, and running after every woman he sees. Says him takes a cup of it every morning."

Knowing how adverse her mother was to root medicines, Lizzie did not think it wise to reveal to Hilda that her mother had never taken the potion and never would because the last one that she took almost killed her.

Instead, she said sweetly, "Yes, thank you Miss Hilda, I am sure she is taking it. In fact, she is beginning to feel better already."

Satisfied with the report Hilda continued, resting her hand on her hammer, "Mr. J. is a close man according to talk, but you would likely know best. I wonder if him talk about private matters with you?"

"Yes," Lizzie said, with assurance, "he is a private man but he does talk to me."

"Well," then said Hilda, "he must tell you what's behind all dem trips him take to the parish of St. Elizabeth?"

Lizzie responded promptly, "Mr. J. has plenty of business dealing over that way. He is always looking for new markets for the produce."

"Well," said Hilda, "he might be looking for new markets but it is not only for produce from what I hear. My cousin, Vinnie, tell me that him come over there quite often and that him seeing a widow woman named Mrs. Etlin Fowler. She is an elementary school teacher who own a nice house and few lovely head of cattle. From what I hear she ordered bridal dress and wedding cake."

Lizzie froze.

She tried to breathe but no air entered her lungs. She knew that Hilda was observing her, but there was nothing she could do to hide the shock.

Slowly, Lizzie pulled her hat down over her forehead as though to shade the sun as her mind raced wildly.

She knew Hilda to be a respected and honest, church-going woman who would not lie to her.

She recalled that St. Elizabeth was her original home parish. Snatches of sentences, fragmented remarks drifted into her head: Mr. J's frequent trips to the post office, letters kept under lock and key, his sheepish looks as he took off in his car. These and other disparate bits and pieces of information flashed before her.

Hilda comfortable with the silence, knew that the news had to be given time to sink in.

She returned to the task of cracking the stones into pieces of crystalline pellets that splintered off into the air.

Could this man be so wicked as to be planning something and not tell her, Lizzie thought.

The question hung in the heavy, hot, stifling air.

Then she heard herself say, "Mr. J. did tell me that he had to go to St. Elizabeth on business."

She paused and continued almost in a murmur, "I keep myself busy with the house and with the books. I notice a lot of packages from St. Elizabeth but I don't pay them no mind."

"Well, child, you should have paid them mind for new wife liable to clean house with new broom."

That said, Hilda gave a decisive hit to the stone she had carefully positioned revealing silver, grey metallic veins that lay shimmering in the sun.

Lizzie made her goodbyes and continued to walk down the road only this time more slowly.

Her body which had been relaxed, supple and flowing earlier felt tight and stiff now. She felt a spasm in her shoulder and wondered what it meant. She tried in vain to integrate the information she had just received, but she couldn't.

Why would Mr. J. do this?

Why would he do this without telling her, she thought, after all she had done for him.

What an ungrateful man!

He had made advances to her from the first time he met her and had given her gifts indicating affection. She, in turn, had become his helpmate.

The agony she now felt made her voice a heavy sigh as she shook her head and murmured,

"Oh! God. Water more than flour!"

She pursed her lips tightly as her eyes stung with tears. She had laid herself open for this.

Yes, the man was a lizard. Who knows what his true color is.

For the past three years she had not only kept house for Mr. J. she had kept Mr. J. himself. Many a night she had held him close to her in his bed. In sickness and in health she had cared for him.

She was a housekeeper, of course, but what they had shared had gone beyond mere housekeeping.

Commitments had been made.

The pit opening up in her stomach grew deeper. What was she to do?

Lost in her own thoughts she did not even realize that she was approaching the district square. Suddenly, she found herself facing Oswald, her cousin.

Wild and crazy Oswald, he was the artist and musician of the family. He spent his days and nights dancing and making music. Lizzie was in no mood to talk with him today.

But with a perceptiveness that goes back to a shared childhood, Oswald observed her closely and said, "What is wrong?" Before she could say "Nothing," he looked deep into her eyes and commanded, "Tell me."

Lizzie's cousin was dressed carelessly in loose working man's clothes; his shirt was open to his waist revealing a body which was well-exercised and excellently toned. After all, he was one of the best folk dancers in the region. During tourist season, he made lots of money and always remembered to send generous gifts to herself and to his Aunt Edna.

Now instead of being joyous and carefree as was his way, Oswald was looking at her and scowling.

Lizzie struggled to look away, trying to shrug things off and show a brave face. In actuality, she was relieved to share with him the news she had just heard.

"The damn little ram-goat!" Oswald murmured under

his breath.

"So what you gwine do Lizzie?" he asked.

"I don't know. I will leave, of course, but …"

"Well, well, well Mr. James, Oswald murmured, you can't be allowed to treat my family member this way."

He continued, rubbing his chin with a slow, circular motion. Lizzie looked at him expectantly, yet nervously.

Suddenly, his face brightened and he threw back his head and laughed heartily.

Looking at Lizzie with magnetic intensity, he said: "Leave it to me, cousin, we will teach that damn mongoose a lesson or two. Leave it to me."

Oswald hugged Lizzie and turning away quickly before she could make further enquiries, called one of his pals, Duppy-Boy, a Rastaman, who was known to sit for hours in deep meditation seeking ways to make the wicked pay for their misdeeds. Together, the two young men moved off into the shade of the darkened alley.

Lizzie felt drained. Her hat was not offering her the shade she needed. There was not a stir in the air, not even a breeze. Beads of perspiration appeared on her forehead. She began an even slower lifeless walk away from the square.

All of a sudden, Lizzie stopped dead in her tracks. She thought, I don't want any trouble. Lord, I hope that's not what Oswald has in mind. She knew that Oswald had good sense, but could she trust it?

As Lizzie turned into the gate of Mr. James's residence,

she saw Alvin relaxing on the porch, bold as day, catching the breeze; the cutting of the hedge and the weeding of the flower bed were left unfinished.

He was a fresh-mouthed boy, and she had intended to ask him to leave the porch immediately and return to his duties, but thought better of it and asked the whereabouts of Mr. J.

Alvin answered with an impudent smile, "You work here longer than me, you should know. Me no follow him 'round. Him at him duties, keeping the peace!"

Alvin picked up a dry twig and started chewing on it, smiling slowly and insolently while keeping his gaze on Lizzie.

She would have had a ready answer for him, to silence him and put him in his place, but not today, she had bigger fish to fry.

"And" continued Alvin, sensing weakness and pressing home his advantage, "Mr. J. want you to cook up red bean sauce over white rice and jerk chicken, vegetable, plantains and some fried fish with onions, I recommend a couple a nice pieces of grouper fish."

Of course, he had included a couple of his favorites, but Mr. J. won't mind, he thought. Then as an afterthought, he added, "Someone might be coming back with him for dinner tonight."

This was too much for Lizzie, the blood rushed to her head, and whirling to face him she said, "Boy, I don't take orders from you. I am a big woman and you are but a boy hardly out of short pants. You and Mr. James want food?

You both go and cook it. I cook nothing more here. So you get out of my way, you hear me?"

Alvin shocked by the sudden blast, wilted and backed away.

No dinner tonight by the look of things, he thought. What the hell, happened, he asked himself, for he too, liked Lizzie's cooking.

Lizzie went to her room and quickly began to pack her things. She took care to leave behind several of the small gifts Mr. J had given her. She may not be rich but she did not need anything from this wicked man.

In the office, at the court house, Mr. James settled back into his chair, exhausted. Hearing the different stories from all the members of the Huggins family had taken most of the day. Yes, the Huggins were a warrior tribe; most likely Ashanti. Dealing with them demanded the patience of Job if not the Lord, himself. Yet, he had persevered and settled the dispute. Well, not exactly settled in a strict sense. A truce had been called. Blood could still be shed, he knew that.

However, Sammy Huggins agreed after tearful pleas from his daughter that the despised son-in-law, Ned, be allowed to take a specified amount of coconuts, bananas and yams from the land on specified days; not for sale but for home use only.

This was problematic since everyone knew how speedily

his daughter's family had increased and that extra money was needed to maintain the household. Market sales always beckoned.

At one point in the hearing, Mr. James stood at his most erect and gave the family a lecture on the importance of honesty and integrity, cautioning them not to resort to force of any kind, violence or threats but to rely instead on reason and on religion.

Reluctantly, family members agreed to restrain themselves more because they were hungry and worn-out from the day's proceedings than by a firm belief in pacifism and high principles.

By design there had been no lunch break.

Still, satisfied and well-pleased with his success, the Justice of the Peace sent the Huggins clan to their homes with his blessings and went to his car for the drive into the district center.

As Mr. James's car entered the square, he noticed that the atmosphere was unusually festive. Strains of music filled the air as musicians showed off their abilities. The sound of drums and rumba boxes thundered out the anchoring beats that allowed the banjoes and guitars to soar.

Boys and girls were moving to the rhythms and cadences of the songs while sounds of women's laughter floated out over the fields. The air was sweet with frangipani flowers.

Why such jubilating and dancing, Mr. James wondered.

Has the government been giving out money gratis? He shook his head, but remembering that the day's post had arrived, decided to call once more to see if there was any more mail for him and to stop in at the general store for cigars and the like.

He was expecting a guest and looking forward to being notified of her arrival.

As he approached, the crowd began milling around the musicians. Mr. James parked and exited his car but could not help noticing that several furtive glances were cast in his direction. He ignored them. Rabble, he thought, just crowding up the place.

He thought of his friends who lived on the outskirts of town in the lovely homes on the surrounding hill and thought it time to pay them a visit.

Then, suddenly, the music exploded. Fifes led off the piece, followed by banjos and guitars with drums playing a lively backup and Oswald began to sing:

Verse 1:

Me say, Man; Me say Man;
Me say yeah, yeah man!
Body up, Body up,

Me got a little tale to tell
A tale 'bout someone you know quite well
Him know how to count, and him know how to spell
But Lord knows, dis man ain't no angel;

Him sit in session, and him take possession
Him talk of the law and him talk of the land
But come evenin' time, he's a cunning man
Him draw down whatever he can;

Chorus:

Lordy, Lordy he's a cunning man
Drawing down whatever he can (repeat).

Verse II

Some say he's a rhetorician
Some say he's a theoretician
But I say that he's a mathematician
And he knows how to add two and two;

But two women a house will cause you trouble
Two as a rule will make you grovel
Admit that you are a louse and a mockery
So say the people and we're the jury.

As the music rang out, the crowd began to stomp, clap and sway to the rhythm with the music. Duppy-boy who was playing the banjo offered a cadenza and the crowd danced with wild abandon.

Mr. James felt decidedly uneasy and uncomfortable.

He decided to return to his car and drive home to escape the loud music and rowdiness of the crowd.

Was the derision in the song intended for him?

What could be worse in life than to end up in a popular calypso, sung with as much improvisation as desired by every lewd boy on the street?

How could these ignorant people know his business? He has always been a private man. A very, very private man.

As Mr. James entered his own driveway and parked his car, he noticed Lizzie standing on the veranda.

He didn't like her looks. What did she know?

The queasiness in his chest told him that she knew something. He looked at her again and knew that she knew everything!

How was he going to face her?

He had planned time and time again to talk over the matter with her, about his personal plans, but had run out of time.

Lizzie read Mr. J.'s face and knew without doubt that what she had heard was true.

She stood still, arms folded, hardly breathing, and watched him leave the car, pick up his brief case and walk slowly toward the front steps.

It was then they heard in the distance the approaching strains of sweet calypso music wafting gently in the air.

The musicians and their entourage were playing from the back of a pick-up truck which was being driven ever so slowly up the road.

Lizzie heard the sweet, sweet music and could pick out Oswald's voice from a composition that had now taken on a lead and chorus orchestration.

Lizzie saw Mr. James wince as he turned his head to catch the lyrics. The throbbing rhythms of the calypso played on relentlessly as verse after verse of the song was reworded and improvised.

Mr. J. looked around as though for assistance. He glanced at the garden only to see that the fool-boy, Alvin, had dropped his gardening tools and was enjoying the festivities, dancing to the music, winding up his backside like a damn treacherous snake.

Lizzie took a deep breath and felt the pain in her chest begin to ease. She smiled triumphantly.

In her heart, she thanked her cousin.

As the musicians came closer and stopped in front of the gate to pick her up she recognized her friends.

Lizzie felt her spirit soar and her heart swell with pride. She almost felt like doing the victor's dance in defiance. But she did not. Instead, she stood up, picked up her bag and slowly began to descend the steps, brushing her body lightly against her former employer as she passed.

Mr. James groaned and steadied himself by gripping the railing by the steps. Life without Lizzie flashed before his eyes. Life without Lizzie … Life without Lizzie was unthinkable!

Looking at her longingly, he reached out and said: "Lizzie I can change my mind. The future should have been clearer to me than it has been ... the implications and ramifications of my actions were not perceived at the time. However, after all this tribulation, if only we could re-ignite the flames ..."

But Lizzie had had enough. Her mind was made up.

She turned to him and said: "You talkin' but I can't hear you, Mr. J. All I hear is this sweet calypso music. Listen to it, for you will be hearing a lot of it. Maybe it'll go to #1 in the music chart."

Danny's Marbles

"A man should not be living too long in his mother's house," Danny Hodges said to himself as he opened his eyes and knew himself to be awake. Not one to lie abed too long, he eased himself off the thin mattress and looked about the small room that he knew to be his as though he was seeing it for the first time. The morning sunlight was peeking through the broken slates of the wood paneling along the side across from his bed. This was his mother's house and he knew it.

He could hear the pots and pans rattling in the kitchen. She was cooking. The kitchen, more a shed than a house, was shared by all the members who lived in the yard; some were family members, others were renters who had moved in to the compound and needed a place to cook.

Danny knew that his cousin, Gertie, would be there. She was an early riser and always started the day's meals at this time with his mother, Anna, who was her aunt.

Danny looked around the room, his eyes still adjusting to the brightness of the sunlight pouring through the jalousie window he had opened. He could hear his mother's and Gertie's voices more clearly now.

Gertie was saying that the best thing about a funeral was the festivities that accompanied it. She will be going to the wake following the funeral of Mrs. Aiken this afternoon up at Nine Mile.

It had been two years since there had been a good funeral in the community. A funeral with a rich wake where there would be plenty to eat and drink.

Danny heard his mother chuckle and say, "This is going to be a good one. Already they have begun to dig the grave and set up the tables and the counters at the house. The corpse lived abroad in foreign for many, many years; some people say as much as forty years before comin' back here. Like so many other of dem people, she discover that America was a good place to make money but not to live. Not to live, man! Over there, there was only hard work day after day, and a lot of cold weather and something they call snow. So Mrs. Aiken decided to return home to build herself a nice home in the end to be buried right here."

Gertie agreed and added, "Maybe she no have no friends over there in that cold place and she miss her roast bread-fruit, bammy, codfish and the like."

Anna laughed ironically and said, "Maybe, she also miss family and can't give up the island."

Gertie quickly added: "But if I could get some of the money I hear there is in America, me wouldn't mind takin' the cold."

Anna who had scrubbed one of the pots with a coconut

brush and was filling it with water for the rinse, responded, "What you know 'bout cold weather? At Christmas time, just a little chill and you put on every piece of clothes that you got and also some of mine."

All laughed in unison for they know that Aunt Anna was right. Gertie was always the first to complain about what she called cover-up weather.

Satisfied that her point had been made, Anna quickly changed the subject and returned to the arrangements for the upcoming funeral mentioning the names of the people she heard would be doing the cooking and what was to be prepared. Everyone was looking forward to being richly provided for at the wake.

Danny listened to the conversation without registering much of what was being said. His mother and Gertie always talked together … day after day.

He listened to their voices as he would to the rustling of the leaves or the rattling of tin cans. He reached for his pants which he quickly pulled on, but decided to stay in his undershirt as it made him feel cooler in the coming heat of the day.

The chatter went on but he had lost the thread of the conversation. Slowly, he put his head in his hand and rubbed it as though there was something he was trying to remember but couldn't, no matter how hard he tried. The throbbing at the back of his skull began again but he ignored it. This was going to be just another day.

He walked out of his room through the communal area of the house on to the steps. There he sat down exactly as he had the day before and the day before that.

From this place, he could watch and listen to all the activities in the yard without being a participant. Listening and watching were things he did very well. Family members would encourage him to join in but he seldom felt so inclined.

Anna decided to review the background of the Aiken family.

She explained that it was Mrs. Aiken's money that had rebuilt that family house at Nine Mile where she was raised as a child and where some members of the Aiken family still lived. Several of the Aiken's clan had gone abroad but one by one they came home.

Now, Mr. Tom, Mrs. Aiken's nephew, who had recently returned from England, occupied the house. It is said that Mrs. Aiken would be buried on the piece of land near the house where her parents and the rest of the family had been buried.

Grandfather Baba declared that he had known Mrs. Aiken when he was young and she had been a good-looking woman. A bit proud, but still a good looking woman with a fine figure.

He explained further, that Mr. Tom actually lived in two different houses, one in the country and one in the city. When he was tired of one he would just move to the other. People with money do things like that, he explained.

There was silence until Gertie volunteered, with a rueful smile, that she knew why Mr. Tom needed two houses for she had seen him up there lots of times with his neighbor's daughter, Miss Bernice, walking on the veranda.

Anna knew as much but hushed her mouth. Baba laughed derisively, scratched his head, but said nothing. Gertie continued, "I hear his wife is from foreign … nice English woman, I hear, very kind."

Both women laughed again and glanced at each other, "But she live in the city …" Anna noted.

Suddenly, Anna looked up and saw Danny sitting in his usual place on the steps. "Oh! You up, now, young man!"

She threw out the water in the freshly rinsed pots on to the meager vegetable garden outside the kitchen door.

"I will soon bring you tea."

She took three large crackers out of a bag near the pot, poured a steaming hot cup of mint tea which she took to the small table beside the house. She motioned to Danny who left the steps to sit down to have the morning's repast.

As he ate, Danny looked around the yard at the large poinciana tree full of red blooms, the dried banana stalk hanging off the plant, the green bushes growing by the edge of the yard and the patch of obligatory strong-scented mint by the side of the front door.

The rubbish heap was there, well hidden but he knew where it was. It didn't smell but it was unsightly all the same. No one quite knew what to do with it. From time to time someone would simply burn it.

Danny ate absent-mindedly, seeming not to taste what he was eating or to find anything remarkable in the scene he looked at every day.

Anna began to sing as she swept the yard, and as she swept the words of one of her favorite hymns came to mind. One she had learned as a child in Sunday school many years ago.

Jesus loves me this I know, for the Bible tells me so
Little ones to him belong, we are weak but he is strong,
Yes, Jesus loves me, Yes, Jesus loves me
Yes, Jesus loves me, for the Bible tells me so …

The other verses she could not remember. She simply hummed the melody. Danny found her singing comforting and cocked his head as though following along. He smiled and nodded at his mother.

Anna looked up at her son and said, "Well, Danny we going out to a wake this evening, boy. Good time, this evening! Nothing better than a good wake after a funeral. Mrs. Aiken is being buried at Nine Mile and we all going."

Danny asked if they were going to church. "No church," his mother, said, "just the festivities. You will have good time: music, food, rum, everything." She laughed good-naturedly.

That evening Anna laid out clean pants and shirt for her son. After Danny was dressed, together with Gertie and several others they set out for Nine Mile.

Baba said it was too far for him to a walk. He didn't see well at night anymore either. He would stay home and rest himself. They can bring some of the good food.

By the time the family got to the wake, the musicians

were laying out their instruments, the pots were already on the fire and the cooks were checking the blaze.

The onlookers could smell the food as it cooked: goat head soup with vegetables and ground products, known as *mannish water* (everyone knew that it worked to increase virility in men), stew tripe, jerk chicken, mutton with okra, rice and peas, yams, sweet potatoes and fried plantains.

The aroma wafting through the air made everyone heady. Quickly the crowd of mourners began to build.

Danny, in addition to members of his family and friends, watched as several cars and vans drove up and parked followed by a large bus out of which came many well-dressed persons, all attired in black or white clothing.

Having concluded the church service, the next of kin and friends of the family led by the minister walked a short distance to the grave site where the ceremonies were to be held. The singing and the testimonials went on for some time before the body was interred.

Unlike the bawling and hollering heard at the typical local funeral, there was some groaning and sighing at this one but very few tears. After all Mrs. Aiken was 95 years old when she passed, and all agreed that she had lived a rich and full life.

Many of the mourners had come from foreign parts: America, Canada, England, other Caribbean islands and from distant places within the island itself. They were all well-educated people, and well-educated people don't carry on like that ... hollering and screaming. They only sigh and dab their eyes.

Of course, there was some tension in their midst for Mr. Tom's foreign wife had come up from town for the funeral. His secret mistress and neighbor in the country, pretty Miss Bernice was also in attendance and she was dressed quite attractively in black.

No one knew what to do about her presence. But she knew Mrs. Aiken too, after all.

There was lots of glancing and finger-pointing so that those who did not know could be informed of the situation … but no one knew what to do.

Finally, the foreign woman went up to the mistress faced her front and center and told her to her face that she had a nerve to show her face considering that she was a whore and a marriage-wrecker.

She dressed down Miss Bernice, something terrible, by including a few choice Jamaican obscenities that made the eyes of the locals pop.

For a white foreign woman she was very well-informed. The sympathy of the crowd flowed to her. After all she was a wife. Respect was due.

Embarrassed and shamed before her peers, Miss Bernice withdrew and made a hasty departure to everyone's relief.

Mr. Tom, however, pretended not to notice the drama. He appeared to be deep in conversation with a couple of his men friends and so took no stand one way or another.

The resolution of this intolerable situation was left for another day.

After the grave site ceremony was over, those in charge

set up the table with the liquor … and there was plenty of it.

There was white rum, spice rum, golden rum, coconut rum whatever kind of rum you could want, all recognizable brand names and labels. Of course, soda and lemonade were available for the children.

Soon the crowd was invited to partake of the table and in a short time everyone who was thirsty had a paper cup full of rum in hand along with ample food on a plate in the other.

The musicians began to play and the good times began.

Several persons kept going up to members of the immediate family, especially those who came from abroad and looked like they had money, to announce that they were distant relatives. From time to time, money changed hands and a multitude of thank-you's could be heard.

Anna and Gertie made sure that Danny was well provided for in that, besides food, he had a couple of drinks and they were not mild sodas.

More and more people joined the outdoor festivities, but the cooks were prepared and the food and liquor kept flowing.

There were some complaints, murmured by the locals in the district, however, that people from outside the village to whom the wake did not rightly belong were boosting the numbers. But as long as there was plenty of food and drink, all was well.

Anna exchanged courtesies with her neighbors and

friends and had a couple of extra plates made to take home for Baba.

She looked around for Danny but he was nowhere to be found. She asked Gertie if she had seen him and Gertie, already floating from the generous cups she had taken from the liquor table, and the amount of goat stew she had eaten, was not focusing.

Anna persisted with her query and finally Gertie's eyes found Danny mixing in with the crowd, laughing and talking with everyone. At the sight, Anna looked nervously at Gertie who calmed her and told her that everything was alright.

Anna agreed and decided to have another spiced rum punch and talk with a couple more friends.

Suddenly, she felt an internal tug and thoughts of Danny popped into her head.

She scanned the crowd again for him again. This time, she watched as Danny began his approach to one of the well-dressed women from foreign.

She was an attractive woman wearing a fine black dress tightly fitted at the waist and richly embroidered with tiny pearl buttons.

Danny smiled at her with delight, whispered something in her ear, placed his arms around her waist in a familiar way, pulling her close as he toyed with the tiny bead-like buttons that went down the back of her dress.

Anna leapt to her feet and rushed toward Danny. By the time she reached him, the woman had backed away. She had graciously but firmly extricated herself from Danny's arms and, looking at him in a puzzled way, had enquired if he were a relative.

Danny began to follow her laughing with pleasure and tried again to reach for her, but before he could touch her, Anna intervened, grabbed him by the arm and quickly pulled him away. Others immediately claimed the attention of the woman.

Danny was in good spirits, but his mother's appearance dampened his joy. He told her that he wanted to speak with the pretty woman with the little buttons just a little more. He wanted to tell her ... Anna ignored his request and declared that it was time to go home.

Danny resisted and tried to break away, looking back longingly at the woman, but with Gertie's assistance they managed to get him away from the crowd.

They sat him down firmly and began to gather up their belongings for the journey home.

Before their departure, Anna enquired about the woman from foreign in whom her son had shown such keen interest. She learned that her name was Jennifer, Mrs. Aiken's niece, god-daughter and heir.

She wasn't really foreign for she had been born local but had lived abroad for many years. She returned to the island frequently in later years to visit her aunt and had now returned to handle funeral arrangements.

As the group walked back to the house in the darkness, Anna talked of all the good food and the free drinks they had and asked Danny if he had had a good time. He agreed, but mentioned that most of all he liked the lady in the dress with the small buttons.

Anna listened, without emotion.

Then, out of curiosity, she asked him what he had whispered to this woman from foreign whom he favored so much. He said slowly, "I told her that I really loved her and I wanted her and I wanted her to come with me"

Anna looked at Gertie but no one said a word. They walked the way home in a silence broken only by Anna's humming of her favorite hymn under her breath.

When they reached the house, Anna watched her son prepare for bed as she mixed the medication the doctor had prescribed for him. She knew that he often cried and called out in his sleep at night and she wanted to make sure that he rested well. She put in a little extra medication in the glass and stood there while he drank every last drop. He took the medicine without resistance.

Before long, the group at the grave site began to thin as the mourners began to bid each other fond farewells and to re-enter their cars and vans for the journey back to town.

Jennifer, exhausted by all that had taken place, chose to be driven back to her hotel by her cousin, Ben, a man in whose presence she felt comfortable. He would be the one to help her during the next two weeks on the island as she wrapped up her god-mother's business affairs.

Upon entering his car, she adjusted the seat to her body, stretched out her long legs as far as they would go, laid her head back on the headrest of her seat and felt for the first time the weight falling from her shoulders.

The finality of the burial began to hit her.

Her god-mother was gone and she was left with memories. This woman had been like a mother to her.

She had mixed emotions: pain and sorrow, but also thanksgiving. Mrs. Aiken had lived a good life. There was no doubt where she was going.

Jennifer sighed and began a review of the day's events. The pastor had delivered a strong eulogy relating her god-mother's exemplary life and her abundant contribution to the church community.

She, Jennifer, had delivered an impassioned presentation on Mrs. Aiken's seminal role in the family highlighting the positive influence she had on everyone.

There was good music and a beautiful casket. Nothing had been spared. The reception after the interment was most generous, abundant and well-managed.

Jennifer's thoughts drifted to the people who had attended the funeral, relatives and friends from far and near.

What a turn-out there was. What a send-off. Her god-mother would have been pleased and proud.

Jennifer thanked all the mourners in her heart.

Closing her eyes, she tried to relax more fully.

Suddenly, she appeared puzzled as she recalled the episode

of the man who had placed his arm around her, clasped her by her waist and tried to pull her close to his body.

Something about this gesture took her by surprise and shocked her. She had found him too forward. Had he been drinking?

With her head still on the rest, she turned to her cousin and told him of the incident, described the man and asked if he knew him.

Ben did not answer at once. Jennifer repeated her question and asked Ben directly, "Who was that man? Is he connected to the family?"

Ben hesitated, dimmed his head-lights at an approaching car and when safely past the vehicle, said, "Oh! Danny, Danny, poor Danny. Danny has lost his marbles. No, he is not related to us. They just let him out of the asylum where he was committed for ten years for murdering his woman, Missy."

Jennifer lifted her head off the rest and fixed her eyes piercingly on him ...

Ben continued, "You see, he had traveled abroad to America as part of the Farm Work Program and had worked hard and sent back every dollar he made to Missy to save for him so that when he came home they could build a home, get married and live a proper life.

When he returned home, there wasn't a penny. Missy had gotten herself a new man and had squandered all the money. Everything was gone. Every last penny!

When Danny realized this, he became distraught. In truth,

he lost his marbles. He and Missy came to blows. During the fight, he grabbed her by the waist, stripped her naked and plunged his knife into her chest. She died instantly."

Jennifer gasped ... and tried to say something ...

But Ben continued, "Danny didn't try to run for he was too far gone by then. His mind had left him.

At the hearings, although there was no doubt that he had committed the act, he was found to be too mentally incompetent to stand trial.

Further, there were extenuating circumstances such as Missy's betrayal of trust and the lack of premeditation.

Danny was assigned to a mental institution where he received treatment. After ten years, it was decided that he would not regain his mental capacities. He was released last year and now lives with his mother and his other relatives up at Curry road.

I was surprised to see him at the wake today. What did you say, he said to you?

Now, it was Jennifer's turn to remain silent.

She placed her head back on the headrest and stared straight ahead. A tremor went through her body.

All she could see were his opaque eyes and the sound of his cooing voice in her ear, "You're so beautiful, such a nice, nice lady, a pretty lady. I want to hold you. I want to touch you ..."

Again, Ben addressed Jennifer, "What did he say to you?'

Jennifer heard herself saying lightly, "He might have

said something, but I can't recall what it was."

She looked straight ahead as brief refractions of light from the star-filled sky flashed off the dark hood of the car as it sped swiftly through the night.

Spirit Forms

Doris sat cross-legged on her high stool behind the glass case in the place of her employment, Mandini's. Her short skirt rose well above her knee displaying a fine pair of dark legs. Her mind was not on work today. She looked out through the wide-open doors of the store onto the busy street where traffic flowed as in a blur.

She looked around the shop and was only vaguely aware of the rolls of cloth on the shelves, the ready-made dresses hanging on racks and the display of local straw and wood-carved handicrafts so fancied by tourists.

Usually, she would be moving around the store checking stocks, straightening up to show Mrs. Durrie, the owner and manager, that she was attentive to business.

Today, she just sat and watched the shoppers come and go, speaking only when spoken to, offering little inducement and encouragement. Her mind was occupied by her own private thoughts. Mrs. Durrie, preoccupied with her ledgers, paid little attention.

Doris asked Mrs. Durrie to permit her to leave early

today. She hadn't said exactly why, but offered the same general reason she had given to her Aunt Etty the night before.

Doris told her boss that she had received an urgent call from her cousin, Cynthia in White Sands, asking her to come quickly.

Everyone knew that when a close family member called in crisis, attention must be paid.

Doris had indicated further that she would like to catch the 4 o'clock bus from Parade.

Although the bus was always late, she wanted to arrive on time in the hope of getting a seat. Her boss had nodded in agreement without further question; a tribute to Doris' diligence and excellent work habits.

Aunt Etty was another matter. Aunt Etty, the relative with whom Doris lived since her mother passed away when Doris was a small child, was more inquisitive and probed for more information; but Doris offered the quite reasonable explanation that her meeting with Cynthia would reveal the problem. Aunt Etty could not gainsay that and so dropped the point.

Etty, a matronly woman, plump with a kindly air about her, was pleased with her niece's position as clerk in a fine downtown store with as good a reputation as Mandani's.

All the tourists by the bus-load and the local upper-class people frequented this store. To her mind, the merchandise was of inordinate expense. She could buy nothing in that store but relished Doris' gifts to her from time to time when there was a sale.

Etty felt that Doris, with her charm and good looks, was in an excellent position to make contacts and get exposure.

Who knows what this could lead to? Who knows?

So far, all had gone well. She encouraged Doris' steady work habits and did not like this "leaving work early and coming home late" business. This was not good for a young woman.

A reputation must be guarded if a good marriage is to be made. Who wanted used goods or even imagined used goods?

Cousin Cynthia lived quite a distance away.

Doris told Aunt Etty that she would take a bag with her in case she missed the return bus and had to spend the night with Cynthia. Etty preferred to have her home, but short of that, felt that she would be safe with Cynthia. She knew that her husband, Marse Joe, would agree with her.

Etty was a careful woman. Smart, yet very superstitious.

She said to her niece, "Get back home as soon as you can. You know that Cynthia can go on and on … Marse Joe don't want me to leave food on the stove too late. You be careful now, girl. Lloyd, down the road, said him see a figure in white walking slow, slow, down the road ahead of him the other night. When him reach it and try to say good evening, the figure disappeared. You best watch you'self gal."

Doris was fully aware of the anxiety her Aunt was trying so valiantly to hide. She took ghost stories seriously and was always talking about people seeing things.

Doris comforted her as best she could and told her that she would be back tonight; at worst she would spend the night with Cynthia and return home the following day after work. Aunt Etty was comforted and kissed her as a show of trust.

All of these thoughts floated through Doris' head as she absent-mindedly tapped out a light rhythm with her fingers on the glass case in the shop.

A round-faced, smiling woman in a faded pink dress entered the store and interrupted Doris' reveries by asking the price of the coral necklace in the case. Deftly, Doris took out the piece and showed it to the woman, being careful to mention that she thought the necklace would look nice on her and enhance her beauty and that her husband would certainly like it too.

From the casual way the customer handled the necklace, Doris knew that buying it was out of the question, and by the look on her face she also knew that the husband was out of the picture as well.

As the woman left the shop, disgruntled, Doris replaced the necklace, sighed and thought to herself, Lord, the time moving so slowly. Five more minutes. Only five more minutes.

Glancing nervously over the store, she noticed that the manager was still sitting poring over the account ledger adding up the figures. Doris looked at her without really seeing her, waiting for the time to pass. The shop was empty and she prayed that it would remain so.

At exactly 4:00 P.M. Doris slid off her stool and walked nonchalantly past Mrs. Durrie into the backroom where she grabbed her hat and bag.

Sticking her head back in the door she said, "Thank you, Mrs. Durrie. I gone Ma'am."

And before Mrs. Durrie could answer, she ran out the back door. Doris didn't mean any disrespect, but she didn't wait because she knew what Mrs. Durrie was going to say, "Give my good evening to your Aunt and don't be late tomorrow because we have a big shipment coming."

Doris hated to hurry out, because she liked Mrs. Durrie and ordinarily she would have stayed to reassure her, but not tonight. She couldn't talk with anybody tonight. She had much to worry about.

Checking her watch, she thought of running to Parade to be there before the bus arrived, but thought better of it, and reminded herself that the bus was always late ... always, so why run?

Ordinarily, she would have stopped to buy fresh coconut water from one of the vendors or go to the market to make little purchases for her Aunt, such as an extra piece of yam, fresh *callalo* or some *cho-cho* ... but not tonight. None of that tonight.

Sudddenly, a strong gust of wind whisked past her, creating pandemonium on the street. Women's skirts flew up over their heads, men's hats went swirling off into the distance.

Doris had to brace herself and hold on to both hat and bag while stopping briefly in the doorway of one of the stores. Shop awnings were flapping loudly every which way and push-cart operators lowered their heads pushing almost blindly in the street. Loose paper floated everywhere.

Lord, thought Doris, this is a warning. This must definitely be a sign.

A string of obscenities escaped the mouth of an old higgler whose tray holding her precious fruit display had toppled and the fruits were rolling everywhere to the delight of passing children.

Doris resisted the temptation to pick up one of the delicious star apples or mangoes for she knew what the old higgler would say to her not only today but every day hereafter as she walked down that street.

By the time Doris reached the bus station, everyone was in the recovery stage. Vendors and pedestrians alike were re-arranging themselves and their belongings while preparing for another gust, if need be. Doris found a protected spot and waited impatiently for the No. 6 bus. She hoped that it would not be too crowded.

When the bus came, there were only a few seats left even though it had only stopped twice since leaving the depot. The passengers, a mix of clerks, vendors of one kind or another, housewives, looked weary. Most traveled with parcels and enormous bags.

Doris knew what was in the parcels: food stuff such as rice, flour, cornmeal, salt fish and maybe a nice piece of mutton. The women had bought material with which to make clothes for the family, and if there was enough money left over, there would be some mint or sweets for the children.

She knew that she wouldn't get a window seat. All she could hope for was to be comfortable. Seated next to a lean, spare man with few packages, she felt lucky. Settling back into her seat, random thoughts began to drift in and out of her head.

The dominant thought at the back of her mind was still there, but she wouldn't let it come to the surface. She couldn't let it; not yet, for it would break her.

From time to time, she looked out the window; first at the foaming, blue-green Caribbean Sea lapping against the sea wall, and then at the green hill sides sprinkled with thatched and cement block houses.

She looked at the small flower gardens in front of some of the homes and smiled in sympathy with the efforts of the gardeners. She knew the work it took to make a stand against those choking weeds and salty winds.

The air inside the bus began to cool as they left the town behind. By the side of the road, Doris noticed that the pretty *Four O'clocks*, her favorite flowers, were opening on time.

The shadows cast by passersby were lengthening. The sun had begun its slow descent into the west. She felt twilight settling in; the landscape was enveloped in a soft haze.

She felt pensive and surprisingly remembered a short poem taught to her by her high school English teacher, Mrs. Edith McDermott:

It is a beauteous evening calm and free,
The holy time is quiet as a Nun
Breathless with adoration; the broad sun
Is sinking down in its tranquility;
The gentleness of heaven brood oe'r the sea:

Try as she might, she couldn't think of the rest of the poem even though she was made to memorize the entire sonnet and could recite it by heart.

She had been one of the brightest in her class, a favorite of her teachers, and one whom everyone had said showed great promise. She could hear Mrs. McDermott repeating the name of the poet to the class: William Wordsworth.

Doris breathed deeply and thought, Sonny had liked reading too. At his mother's house he had kept every one of his school books and had bought some more besides.

Few people knew this about Sonny, but she knew. She knew him better than anyone else knew him. He was a part of her. She knew that his mother, Miss Manda, couldn't read well and it was he who always read to her.

In fact, Miss Manda did not even bother sending to the Post Office for mail anymore. It was she, Doris who picked up her mail on her way home.

Many a time, Doris had read Sonny's long letters to her or given her messages he had sent. Recently, no letter had arrived from her son in over two months.

A spasm passed through her body and she twisted in her seat as the pain, like a jack-hammer, started in her head. The thin raw-boned man sitting beside her turned sharply.

Doris smiled weakly but reassuringly at him and looked away. She had not seen his face. She had seen Sonny's.

Where are you Sonny? She asked. Where are you?

The bus came to her stop. Clutching her bag and her hat which were both on her lap, Doris navigated her way to the door and carefully came down the steps. As she walked to the edge of the road and looked around, the familiar sights and sounds of the evening greeted her.

Mothers held their naked children under water taps in the middle of the yard washing off all signs of the day's play; old men sat outside brightly colored store fronts laughing, drinking white rum and playing dominoes.

The jerk pork vendors roasted their meats on the coals as they awaited the evening's customers. There were shouts and squeals of laughing children chasing each other, denying the ending of the day. The sun's last sprays of light were richly displayed over land and sea, creating an aura of enchantment.

Doris turned to cross the road and was grateful to see her cousin walking to meet her. Somehow Cynthia's presence always seemed to soothe and make her feel safe.

Cynthia was more than a cousin. She was a sister and a close one at that. Doris remembered private confidences they had shared all through school in a friendship that continued to this day. It was natural for her to ask Cynthia's help with this difficulty.

The two young women embraced each other and absorbed in private conversation, walked toward a small two-storey house which in better days had been painted blue and pink. Now, only a faint memory of the paint remained. The gate and small porch showed several broken slats and loose boards. Doris said nothing for she knew the situation.

Cynthia and her mother had known hard times since Mr. Jackson, a lawyer in town and Cynthia's father, had passed away. Life was never easy for the family because Mr. Jackson was never married to Cynthia's mother. They were what was known locally as a second family.

Mr. Jackson visited when he could and supported as best he could. His first family anchored in law and legitimacy took precedence and priority. Divorce was out of the question. Cynthia and her mother survived as best they could.

As the women entered the door of the house, Doris asked anxiously, "So when we going to go?"

"Not yet, man, not yet!" Cynthia replied hastily.

"We have to eat first and change your clothes and then we go."

Cynthia was an attractive, easy-going young woman who had a way of creating an air of ease and well-being where ever she went.

At the local bakery, where she worked as a cashier, many a handsome young man came to buy fresh baked patties and coco-bread every day whether they were hungry or not. Cynthia was good with people. She had an infectious laugh and a caring way that brought customers back.

She cared deeply for her cousin, Doris, and had often come to her assistance for one thing or another. Of course, no instance was ever as serious as this.

Doris wasn't a weak person but she always had such an

air of helplessness about her when she was in trouble that Cynthia couldn't resist taking charge. It was for this reason that she had told Doris to come tonight.

In the kitchen, Cynthia spread the table, laid out the plates and invited Doris to sit down to eat. She explained that her mother was away in the country visiting her brother, both of whom managed the small parcel of family land her father had gifted them with.

Tonight, Doris wasn't interested in Cynthia's mother. She paced nervously about the room and declined the offered meal, accepting instead a glass of lemonade. Cynthia sat herself down to dinner. There was an air of quiet waiting between them.

Sipping the lemonade, Doris walked out into the yard where she had been scores of times. She checked things out quickly and saw that there was nothing new: the same scraggly vegetable garden, the same large mango tree in the back yard and the same old beaten-up, rust-eaten van that Mr. Jackson had bought for Cynthia's mother eons ago.

Slowly Doris' eyes wandered from the yard and onto the tops of neighboring roofs. She thought of Sonny.

She had first met him at the Sun Splash Festival in Montego Bay two years ago. He had seen her with friends and wanting to meet her had made enquiries. She had agreed to a meeting without any initial hesitation, because she had liked him from the start.

Doris smiled to herself at the memory. Her Aunt Etty had met him and liked him also. But Doris had not shared just how serious things were between them.

Etty liked the fact that Sonny had a good paying job and nice manners. Right off, he began addressing her as "Aunt Etty" which sat well with her.

Doris recalled the walks out by the sea and the long talks they had as she was getting to know him.

Sonny worked on board a cargo ship he had told her, and so he was away for long periods of time. She shouldn't let that trouble her, he had said, because they were bound heart to heart by indestructible bonds of love.

No one would guess it but Sonny was such a romantic. Warm, loving and wonderful.

Doris had given herself to him on a hot evening in July and as they lay in each other's arms, their bodies spent of desire, their faces luminescent with the glow of their passion; she had known that their union was sacred. They knew that marriage would only affirm what already was.

Sonny was right. These feelings were sacred and indestructible. He had given himself to her in a way that she had not known that a man could. He allowed himself to be absorbed by her and to meld with her.

At first she was surprised by their passion, and tried to hold something of herself back. But Sonny broke through the barriers she had raised, hushed her fears and gave even more of himself to her. He had share with her sexually and spiritually in such a way as to let her know that he had held nothing back and neither should she. They were one.

On his return from his trips, Sonny would bring expensive gifts: jewelry, articles of clothing such as dresses, silk scarves and other treasures.

Doris felt content and even though she missed him when he was away. She had hopes for the future and she busied herself with planning and saving as much of her earning from Mandani's as she could.

After all, holding a wedding, not to speak of setting up a home, took real money. Some people held the wedding but couldn't set up house properly because of the number of relatives that had descended on them and had to be fed and entertained during the celebration.

Sonny had said that he planned to open a shop some day and import merchandise. He implied that he had connections abroad. She had envisioned them managing their clothing business together.

She thought of children. The last time she saw him, he had wanted to speak with Aunt Etty about his intentions and to plan for their wedding. Sonny was a good man. She knew that. He was a very good man.

Lost in thought, her body stiff and immobile, Doris did not hear Cynthia come up behind her.

Her cousin had finished supper, washed up and had decided to come out and join her. For a moment neither spoke.

Yet, much needed to be said. Cynthia could read her cousin's thoughts and knew that she had to choose her words carefully.

So placing her hand gently on Doris' shoulder she said, "What you going to do is not goin' hurt Sonny. No. It goin' help you. After all, you have a right to know. Maybe him on his way back to you. Maybe other things are going on.

These days you don't know what kinda business people are in. Drug runnin' heavy in Jamaica now. You have to face up to it, man.

"I'm taking you to Duncan for him can help you. I hate to see you pining away so. Listen to me, Doris, nothing goin' happen to you. When things bad with people 'round here Duncan always help them. My father's wife and family did want to take the house and everything from me and my mother after Papa pass away; it was Duncan who help us. So, come now darlin', change your clothes and let's go."

Doris said nothing because she had made up her mind already. She meant to go through with it. She was going with Cynthia regardless of what happened.

She was going because she had to know. She had to know.

Both women changed their clothes. Doris put on an old dress and the pair of battered closed-up shoes she had brought with her. Cynthia was also appropriately dressed in corduroy pants, a loose top and a pair of old walking shoes.

Satisfied that all was in order, Cynthia picked up the lantern and both women left the house to begin their brisk walk down the road.

Shortly, they turned off the road and on to a narrow path that led into the trees. After fifteen minutes or so they came to the gully. The sunlight was fading fast but there was still enough light with which to see.

Cynthia said, "Be careful, there is a little more water in the river bed than usual because of the heavy rains last week. Step on the stones. Don't fall. Here, follow me."

Doris with her dress held high around her hips was busy pushing the tall ferns away from her legs as she looked for smooth stones on which to place her feet.

As they began to mount the hill they heard the drums. Doris felt the beating resounding through her body.

"Why, they start already?" she asked. "Why they start?"

Cynthia responded quickly, "This evening is not for you alone, you know. It is their gathering. I just ask them if you can come. They're not waiting for you."

After one more turn they approached a clearing. Cynthia lit the lantern and they continued up the hill.

The small halo the light made on the ground revealed a well worn path and, in the distance, a circular hut anchored in the middle by a tall pole.

In front of the hut was a blazing fire, and to the far side of the fire sat the drummers beating out one of the rhythms she had heard echoing down from the hills ever since she could remember.

A single line of white clad figures with white peaked head-dresses began filing out of the hut. Swaying their bodies in long graceful movements to the cadence of the drum, they danced to face the darkness and then to face the light as though the polarities were manifested in them.

Doris began to feel out of place and a bit nervous and for the first time, she wondered if she had done the right thing by coming.

For some reason, her thought went to Aunt Etty, but she put that figure out of her mind quickly. This had nothing to do with Aunt Etty. Aunt Etty was afraid of her own shadow.

Staying even closer to Cynthia than before, she whispered, "What is going to happen?"

"This is the ritual blaze," Cynthia explained. "The first part of the ceremony is beginning."

As the intensity of the drumming increased, the dancers moved with more abandon, quickening their movements. They took turns approaching the fire, each dancing separately and yet the movements appeared to be in unison.

From where she stood with Cynthia, the dancers seemed to be wrapped in a translucent haze. Doris was mesmerized.

At times, she felt as though she couldn't breathe for her breath was constricted in her chest. It was as though she had left behind all that she had known, all those things about which she was certain, and was about to give herself up to the unknown.

Cynthia was drawing her closer now, and Doris could make out the faces of the dancers from the village. There were others she had never seen before. No one looked her way or appeared to notice her.

There was an other-worldliness about the place, about the atmosphere, even about the dancers. Everyone was held as though in a trance.

The rhythm of the drums was changing again. The drummers had settled into one of the old African rhythmic patterns that seem to pre-date time.

The dancers swirled and dipped and rose with the beat.

Out of the dimness of the hut, came Duncan, the ceremony leader, a tall slender yet muscular man. Dressed in white, his head wrapped in a multi-colored turban, he approached the group with a staff in one hand and a goblet in the other.

Turning to face each of the four coordinates, he raised the goblet to his lips and then sprinkled some of its contents on the ground as though to pay tribute to the earth. That done, he approached the circle and it widened to receive him.

Signaling a change in rhythm with this staff, Duncan stepped into the circle. In this new sequence, the drummers pounded out the mythic sounds by alternately hitting and then rubbing the heel of the hand against the taut skin of the drum.

The sounds, guttural and elemental, mimicked sounds sometimes made by storm winds as they moved through the trees, the groaning sounds seemed to emanate from the earth itself.

Duncan began the dance. His movements, austere, stylized were powerful and riveting. The dancers responded to his every movement and motion, lifting and lowering their bodies in rhythmic waves.

As though at a set time, the sound of the drums became muffled. The dancers formed a circle, clapping and the chanting they danced in place.

Duncan, majestic in his sense of himself and in the immensity of his role, danced alone.

His presence and his movements, ageless and timeless had survived centuries of persecution and oppression. The artistry of his movements bore traces and echoes of traditions and ceremonies from the African past, lovingly remembered, held in the dim recesses of the subconscious.

In a deep bass voice he called out to his dancers the phrase to be repeated in unison in the formulaic pattern of a chant.

The group responded. Standing still but swaying where they stood, the dancers/singers watched their leader and seemed to time-travel with him to regions unknown as they danced in the dim light of the night.

The gathering took on the aura of fantasy and dreams.

It was only upon seeing Cynthia in the circle that Doris realized that her cousin was no longer by her side.

She wanted to join the gathering but lacked the courage. The drums sounded in union with the chanting.

The leader sensing that all was ready for the entry of the spirits called out to Dumballah.

Leader: *Dumballah Oh! Dumballah Oh! Dumballah Oh!*
               Master of the Light
               Master of all Life
               Draw us in, Draw us in
               Draw us in, Master,

The days, the nights,
Time and eternity are one to you;
Show us our destiny
Draw us in.

Chorus: *We are one. We are all.*
               Show us the way
               Oh Master of the Cross-Roads;
               Keeper of the seal
               Show us the record
               Draw us in …

The rhythm of the drums was now deep and hypnotic.

Doris felt the energy of the group coursing through her. The drumming seemed to stroke her very soul. Almost, imperceptibly, the leader had danced out of the ring and approached her.

Taking her by the hand, he led her into the center of the circle and drew her close to the flame. She sensed the heat, heard the crackling of the wood and yet her body felt strangely cold.

The dancers were moving into the shadows now as though to give space to Duncan and Doris. The chanting of the chorus expressing love and thanksgiving grew to a crescendo. Slowly, she felt her body moving. She began to sway.

Then, taking a red hot stick from the fire, Duncan, the emissary of the Spirits, held it up to Doris' eyes. Her breathing became labored. She felt her senses begin to swim. Duncan replaced the brand and placed his hands over her forehead. She shuddered and would have fallen to the ground had he not held her securely.

Everything seemed to recede from Doris' awareness.

Time stopped.

She felt herself on the ground but she had no memory of being placed there.

She heard the leader whisper to her, "Where is Sonny? Where is your man, Sonny? Call him to you. Call him!"

Swiftly she felt herself being lifted up and out of her body.

From an elevated place she saw all the members of the gathering in the fire light. She saw the valley and the river. She saw a large expanse of land, the sea, the waterfalls and the forest.

With amazing ease she recalled the lines from the school poem by William Wordsworth that had eluded her earlier:

Listen: The mighty Being is awake,
And doth with his eternal motion make
A sound like Thunder – everlastingly
Dear Child! Dear Girl! that walkest with me here,
If thou appear untouched by solemn thought,
Thy nature is not therefore less divine:
Thou liest in Abraham's bosom all the year;
And worshipp'st at the temple's inner shrine,
God being with thee when we know it not.

Doris felt her essence being pulled toward a tunnel by a compelling energy. Carried by golden streams of light, she felt herself floating, suspended in a state of infinite peacefulness.

No words were needed here. Thought itself was action.

She knew that she had only to think of Sonny and he was there. Propelled by longing, her thoughts went out to her beloved.

She wanted to find him, to be with him.

Random scenes floated swiftly before her. Suddenly, Doris found herself hovering over a pale sea, below her floating in the water was Sonny's body.

Again, she sent her thoughts out to him and this time the body disappeared and in its place was an image created as though by mists and vapors, an image of Sonny as she knew him.

She sensed his presence. She felt his love. Instinctively, she moved to join him, to meld with him.

It was then she sensed Duncan's words coming to her, "Not yet. No! Not yet, gal! You can't follow him where he is. *You must live!*"

Struggling as though to resist his admonition, Doris cried out soundlessly to Sonny, "If you would wait for me, I would come."

This time she did not see him. Instead, she saw again the valley and the gathering below her; she heard herself panting softly. She knew that she must re-enter her body and her world.

It was then she felt the pain.

Her face was wet with tears, her body was contracting and convulsing. Duncan cradled and rocked her gently while the dancers sang a plaintive chant. She knew the words:

Chorus: *Take hold of life and grow strong,*
            It is freedom, for which we long,
            God will tell right from wrong;
            Take hold of life, sister,
            Take hold of life, brother
            Life is the bridge to tomorrow,
            Take hold of life, take hold of life;

            Like the vine that wraps the tree,
            Like the child at its mother's knee,
            Life is given to you and me;

            Take hold of life, sister,
            Take hold of life, brother,
            Life is the bridge to tomorrow,
            Take hold of life. Take hold of life.

As the world swam before her eyes, Doris heard Duncan say, "Sonny love you, gal, but him no want you to follow him. Him want you to *live, gal, live, live, live!!!*"

Slowly Doris opened her eyes and tried to focus her gaze. She felt Duncan but could not see him.

Forms and figures seemed to swim in a haze. She sensed Cynthia's concern but could not reassure her.

In an elevated state of awareness, Doris' senses were acute, especially her hearing. Sounds took on a heightened reality.

She heard the movements of the fireflies, the crickets and the night creatures in the distant valley.

She sensed the exhaustion of the dancers' bodies and the fearful and anxious thoughts of her Aunt Etty at her home in Mount Salem. She knew that Sonny's mother would be coming to see her in a day with news of her son's death.

Doris breathed Dumballah's name!

A gift had been given. A wish granted.

There was no need for fear, no feelings of terror for she knew that time was but a mist to be penetrated. She had felt the enlargement of her spirit, felt the power of the unseen world. She knew herself to be one with all things.

Gradually, the window in time began to close.

Her breathing began to slow and her body felt languid and at peace. Her hearing was losing its piercing acuteness as her vision sharpened.

Doris noticed that the fire had burned low. Duncan, the dancers, the drummers and Cynthia had gathered around her in silence as she rested on the cold, hard, earth looking out at the richly splayed colors of the morning's rising sun.

Sweet Naseberries

Adelle Houghton rolled over in her bed and looked at the child in her makeshift cradle built by her uncle. She was fair as her father, with bright curious eyes. She was a pretty little girl wrapped in her baby sheets.

Adelle felt the softness of her own belly and knew that the lump she had carried for these nine months was lying next to her as a beautiful little girl. The baby had closed her eyes and was sleeping, her little face a picture of tranquility.

Adelle felt her own eyes closing as she joined the little one in the moment and though she wanted to sleep, she could not. Instead, she felt hot tears sting her lids as she remembered what she wished to forget.

What would happen to the new life in the crib? What had happened to the life she had planned?

She had been the premier organist in the church. How had everything gone so awry? She could not return to the church now. The deacons would never accept her or her child.

She had disgraced her family. She, Adelle, had been thought to be the rising star in the district. Now, she was an outcast.

She who had delivered so many talks to the young members of the Christian Endeavors Chapter about shaping a good life, had destroyed her own.

She who had rejected so many suitors who had come calling, because, so thought others, no one was good enough for her.

She who had been envied and of whom the spiteful ones had asked bitterly. "Who does she think she is?"

She had drunk fully of the cup of bitter lemons and of vinegar.

Yet, Adelle had known early who she was. From childhood, she had been told often enough that she was pretty and the villagers had watched her grow into a graceful, beautiful young woman with a willowy figure, charming slender face and long elegant fingers suited for her passion, playing the piano.

Her family had gathered up all discretionary funds to send her to the city to study music, for she had shown an exceptional aptitude for the art. She had practiced on wash-stands and table-tops all day until the family bought her a piano.

Her sister Abigail had taken lessons locally and had practiced with her on the prized instrument, each loving the music as much as the other ... but all knew who had the talent.

Abigail had the love for the instrument, but it was Adelle who had not only the love, but the passion and, most importantly, the talent for music. All knew it.

The family had sent Adelle off and paid the enormous cost for boarding and private lessons in the city. Everyone waited eagerly for her return so as to hear of her progress.

So many times as they walked down the street passersby would often stop to admire Adelle, to compliment her on her looks and on her musical performance and to wish her the best for the future.

Abigail, they hardly noticed at all except to pass basic pleasantries.

Adelle would make every attempt to include her sister in the conversations highlighting her contribution, but no one was really interested. The attention was lavished on her.

The younger sister did not begrudge her older sister's success. In fact, she loved and admired her beautiful and accomplished sister very much and Abigail had often done more than her share of the housework so that her sister could spend more time at the piano, playing within her hearing.

When Adelle took up her first position as junior organist at the local Baptist church, the congregation felt that change had come and they welcomed it.

Everyone knew Mrs. Hine's approach to music and

respected her gifts. The older organist was a traditionalist who focused mostly on the correctness of her notes.

Adelle was different. Her playing was vibrant, energetic and rich with many flourishes. She brought style, flair and magical elements to her music. Her performance was enthralling.

Her slender feet played the bass pedals of the organ with as much skill as her hands. She was one with the instrument. She danced with the organ and the choir and the congregation loved it and tried to match her.

With the guidance of Adelle, the choir mistress ordered new music that tested their abilities, and Mrs. Hall, who always commanded every soprano solo from every score, could not manage the challenging new pieces anymore and gladly passed them to the younger singers.

Adelle always played crisp, clear introductions to the hymns and smiled at the choir mistress when it was time for the voices to fall in. She had learned this technique from the bigger churches in the city where she had interned and was determined to bring the district church up to speed.

Once, Abigail remarked that she knew the Sundays that her sister was at the organ the moment she entered the church yard and heard the music pouring out of the church as her sister played the prelude.

She knew her sister's style, for no one had better control of the foot pedals than she did and no one could apply them so richly and with such assurance.

As Adelle reminisced, the baby began to stir and to whimper in the bassinet. She comforted it by stroking its tiny body with her outstretched hand. Yes, this was her child and now what was she to do with it?

Brigham had left her. Again, tears filled her eyes, but this time she wiped them away quickly as she felt the anger moving within her.

She remembered the day she met him. She was attracted to him right away and when he asked her out, she accepted.

Adelle was interested and impressed, but Abigail, not so much. She was not as easily moved. She advised the wait-and-see approach. She advised caution.

Barry had been invited to address the local community leaders on increased funding for local schools allotted by the government.

Adelle learned later that he was highly placed in the Department of Education with a rising career.

Further, he was handsome, open, and excessively bright and he had paid much attention to her. No one was surprised as everyone knew that Adelle would catch any man's eye.

Barry, as she came to call him, had friends in the neighborhood and returned often to visit them. Many thought that it was really to see Adelle and to go on long walks with her.

He came to church to listen to her play and marveled at her gifts and her dexterity. They had gotten to know each other well, for he had driven her to town on errands and after dining with her had stopped to visit her friends and family members.

In the moonlight, richly scented by jasmine bushes, he had held her in his arms and made love to her.

To him, she was as fragile as a flower and as sweet as naseberries.

He told his family about her and especially, his sister, Margaret, whom he trusted.

Brigham's passion for Adelle grew. She returned his love and within the year; he wrote to her family to ask for her hand in marriage.

Her father, a former deacon in the church and a man more given to reading than to planting crops, had passed away the year before and the family was greatly weakened by his loss.

Mother Houghton eagerly gave her consent to the match as she felt that her husband would have agreed.

After all, Barry was a well-educated, young man who presented himself very well. He was friendly, outgoing, charming, and besides had a successful career ahead of him in government. Moreover, he loved her daughter and was attentive to her. Adelle was her favorite child and certainly she deserved the best.

Abigail and Adelle conversed as sisters will about her new love. With the curiosity of a caring and protective guardian, Abigail wanted to know what had passed between them. She knew that on several occasions, Adelle without her mother's knowing had slipped away to meet with her lover many an evening..

Abigail was no beauty, but she was practical, smart and hardworking. She did not want to see her sister hurt.

She did not dislike Brigham, but she was watchful. She was on guard.

On one occasion, she boldly said to her sister, "So, you are sure about this man, Adelle? What do we know about his family?"

Adelle had responded that Brigham's father who had worked for the American Fruit Company had died some years ago and his mother lived in Clarendon with his two brothers and a sister. He had taken a photograph of her to show his family and his mother had given her blessing.

Still, Abigail was not entirely satisfied. She was a girl from a small district and the entry of this young man in their lives had turned things upside down.

She was likely to lose her sister to a man she hardly knew and to a world that was strange to her.

"So, what plans you making with him?" Abigail continued, "will he be working in our part of the island or in the big city? Will he get a transfer?

All of these questions should have been posed by their mother, but since the death of their father, Mother Houghton had become more remote. She still oversaw the workings of the small plantation but not much else. It was Abigail who ran the household.

Adelle was too delirious with happiness at her prospects

to worry much about not having met Brigham's family. Barry had assured her as he held her in his arms that all was well, and she believed him.

No other man she had met before compared with him and, further, he offered her the kind of life she wanted.

Now he lived alone, he said, but after marriage she would move in with him and as his prospects improved, for he was up for promotion, he would buy a larger place for them.

Adelle's eyes danced with joy. The thought of living in the big city filled her with happiness. She was pleased to leave country life behind.

Certainly she would apply to be an organist at a city church and she would meet his other family members as soon as wedding plans took shape.

Then, one Sunday after church and family dinner, Abigail noticed that her sister, whose voice always filled the house with so much laughter that one could tell if she were home, had walked a little ways away into the part of the garden that had grown wild.

She was sitting on a rock looking off into the distance, her hands clutching the stone behind her.

Abigail was quick to join her and slowly begin to probe at what troubled her. After all, things were going well. There were no quarrels with Barry and plans were being made for the future. There was plenty of time to finalize arrangements.

What could the matter be? Why was she so troubled and afraid?

Then, Adelle revealed the source of her concern. She

feared that she was pregnant. Abigail showed no sign of fear or anxiety, but she asked, "Have you told Brigham?"

Adelle said no, for until now she was not sure she was. She had visited Miss Ina, the healer in the district whom they had known since childhood and had asked for confirmation and Miss Ina had given confirmation. She was pregnant.

Abigail said, "So, what now? How will Barry take it?"

Adelle pursed her lips and said with conviction; "Things will work out for us. Naturally, we didn't want it now, but …"

A week later when Barry came to visit, Abigail knew that they talked about it for Adelle said that Barry wanted her to have the baby at the hospital and not with Miss Ina in attendance or any of the local midwives. He was firm on a hospital stay for which he would pay.

The status of the marriage was not raised and so Abigail did not enquire. She did not want to make her sister uncomfortable, for she loved her sister better than herself, and so she willed within her spirit that all would be well.

The child grew within Adelle's body and Brigham came to visit as usual, bringing presents. But the visits became shorter and the length of time between them longer.

Abigail could see her sister, ever fragile, beginning to lose weight even as the child grew within her slender body.

Then one day a letter was delivered to Adelle's mother. No one wanted to open it. It sat on the drawing room table until their mother came.

Mother Houghton opened the letter to learn that Brigham was breaking off the engagement.

Adelle screamed and stumbled as she began her fall to the floor. Abigail caught her and helped her to a chair. Everyone feared for the child within her. A cold compress was placed on her forehead and she was led away to her bed.

Her mother wept and said that if her husband was alive nothing like this would have happened. He would have confronted this man who had taken advantage of their daughter and had shamed their house.

After the initial outburst, Abigail never saw Adelle weep.

At first, Adelle wrote to Brigham but received no answer. So she played the piano most days and read. She wrote short commentaries for the Christian Endeavor Youth Group which she would have delivered in the past but now her writings would have no audience.

Sleeping came hard for Adelle but she tried to eat regular meals to sustain the child within her and she went for lonely walks.

Often she simply sat on large rocks and looked out over the fields.

Loving family members and friends brought her fresh fruits and soups with healthful ingredients said to have special powers; for word had gone out that disaster had struck the family and allies were rallying around them.

Many in the community were sorry for the Houghton's. But there were others who sneered and felt that they had been too haughty for their own good and maxims pertaining to the "fall of the proud" was often introduced to support their moral condemnation.

Sometimes the family heard the bitter derisive laughter of the righteous as they passed by the gate along the road. They knew the cost Adelle would pay for her transgressions. They were simply waiting …

Mother Haughton hardly left the house. She saw only very close friends and relatives. The shades were often drawn as though in mourning. The head-man on the plantation took over the managerial responsibilities.

Only Abigail with a fierce pride and head held high went about her business as usual with visits to the shops, stores, markets and church. Many simply avoided her altogether. Others spoke to her without looking her directly into the face.

Adelle bore her life quietly and with dignity for she had a gentle spirit. She did not go out into the community. She hid herself away.

She was not asked back to church to play for the congregation, nor was she invited to participate in any Christian endeavors activities.

Jamaican ladies would not want that sort of person leading the choir, much less being active in the congregation. Truth be known, she was dropped from church membership all together.

Reverend Thomas, once her greatest admirer, had let it be known that her child, when delivered, would not be baptized or christened in the church for it was born in sin.

Adelle did not return to the church. She remained in the house, roamed her private gardens and played the piano daily. Many thought that it was her music that kept her alive. She practiced at the piano morning and evening, learning and mastering new pieces.

The music, often soulful, echoed through the house and flowed out into the road. Sometimes passersby stopped to listen, for it captured their attention as they passed.

It was although the community was on alert. Yet, no one knew exactly what they were expecting. Those who were expecting Adelle to break were disappointed for Adelle did not break.

She bore her child when her time came. Mother Houghton called Ms. Ina to attend to her. After a long labor, a healthy baby girl was born in the late evening at twilight. She gave out a lusty cry announcing her presence in the world.

All this is in the past, Adelle thought, as she opened her eyes and again looked at the child closely. This is now.

The present vied with past for space in her head. Sometimes she felt that she did not have the strength to move her limbs.

She was advised not to breast-feed her child for she was too weak. The child would suckle with her cousin Ruth who had also just given birth and who had declared that she had milk enough for two.

The child fussed intermittently but just as easily fell back to sleep. Adelle examined the little thing visually and wondered what would happen now.

What would happen to this child? The tears she had bottled up all these many months streamed down her face.

Poor thing, she thought, with such a strong will to live. As though sending a mental message to the child was not enough, she said, "You are so beautiful, so brave and so unknowing and uncaring about the nature of your entry into the world. You are God's child. He must have a special journey for you."

The young mother smiled as she watched the baby rub her fist against her mouth looking for a finger to suck. She is so determined, Adelle thought, and oblivious to all else. I am sure that she will find her thumb.

Suddenly, she realized that the child had no name. What will we call you? She wondered.

Mother Houghton answered that question quickly enough when she announced that the child would be called Blossom, for she was so fresh, so perfect in all details and so expectant of the future, so ready to grow into whatever she would be.

Mother Houghton loved the child and relished taking care of it. Indeed, the presence of the baby revived her and the matriarch took heart, recalled her own child-bearing years and hoped for happy outcomes.

But Adelle's health did not improve. In fact, it deteriorated. No matter what special health drinks were made from the finest of island herbs, no matter the special teas, the bush baths, the visit to the doctors and to the healers, she could not regain her strength.

As the child grew stronger, the mother grew weaker.

Gossip had it that Ms. Ina, the midwife who had delivered the baby, had made mistakes. She had mishandled the delivery and had harmed the health of the mother.

Maybe she had given the young mother the wrong draught composite at the wrong time. Maybe there was a secret infection.

Family members and well wishers became more fearful as Adelle appeared to be languishing, having, possibly, lost the will to live.

Many thought that she still loved Brigham and was dying from a broken heart.

Whatever the cause, Adelle did not recover from the experience of the birthing-bed.

She drifted around the house more like a ghost than a person. Months later, there was a photograph with an announcement on the wedding page of the newspaper presenting the marriage of Brigham to a woman from the United States.

Abigail did everything she could to keep this from Adelle, but it was small district and sooner or later she saw it.

But Adelle said nothing.

Brigham had also received a promotion in his position and was off to a very lucrative and promising career. He was traveling to England to take a training course. After all, he was an able and talented man who had won the admiration of his peers.

Gossip had it that Brigham was fearful that the birth of his illegitimate child would harm his career prospects as he rose up the ladder.

Jamaica was all about respectability in those days. So, he chose career over true love.

Others thought that he might have gotten the woman he married pregnant also and her family had enough clout to hold him to his commitment. Hence he had no choice.

To this day, no one knows the truth of the story.

Soon after Adelle's death, Mother Houghton passed on.

Abigail loved and raised Blossom as her own. She poured into the child all the love she had for her sister and pledged her life to her.

Since Abigail never married, she gave thanks for the little one who bloomed and flourished before her eyes.

The child grew like a Jamaican naseberry, a fruit rich and gritty, bearing the sweet mixed taste of cinnamon, apple and pear growing on a tree tall and elegant whose roots go deep, deep in to the earth.

Later in life, Abigail traveled abroad and took the child with her. A strong believer in educating women, Abigail gave Blossom every opportunity to grow and to develop her talents.

Quick to learn, ambitious and mystical in her leanings, Blossom matured into a well-educated and much admired woman who achieved a high and distinguished place in the professions. She married well and had family of her own. Known for her generosity and her kindness to others, the fates smiled on her and her children flourished.

She had courageously taken hold of life and lived.

Your life is a never-ending journey
Ever moving forward in its knowing,
Your life ...
Your life has been a precious stone
Rich with inner beauty,
Your life has been a beacon
Guiding those lost at sea,
Your anchor resting at great depths
Holds them firm, yet free; ...
You have learned, you have grown
And you have shone.

About the Author

Barbara Paul-Emile is an award winning author of fiction and visionary poetry. Born and raised in Springfield, a district ten miles from Montego Bay, Jamaica, she has written creatively since childhood. Barbara Paul-Emile's fiction and poetry, inspired by the rich mystical heritage of Caribbean island culture, has appeared in American and Canadian journals. Her voice in Caribbean literature is said to be "an original one with strong cross-cultural appeal." Her novel, *Seer* (Sunstar Publishing) winner of the *Chelson Award* for fiction appeared in 2004 and her collection of visionary poems: *The Dance of Life: Poems for the Spirit* (Eunoia Press) accompanied by a CD was published in April, 2005. Described as "an exciting literary voice who chronicles the richness of the multicultural experience," Dr. Paul-Emile was selected by the Women of Harvard Club Committee as an honoree for demonstrated leadership and outstanding achievement at their 3rd Annual Boston's Most Influential Women's Award Ceremony, 2014.

Barbara Paul-Emile is the inaugural Maurice E. Goldman Distinguished Professor of Arts and Sciences and Professor of English at Bentley University. She was elected to Phi Beta Kappa at New York University and holds a Ph.D. from the University of Colorado – Boulder. Dr. Paul-Emile's work centers on 19thc English Romantic Literature, Myth, and Caribbean Literature. She was a member of the faculty at CU, Vassar College, and Associate Director, and later Research Fellow, Radcliffe Institute of Advanced Study, Harvard University.

Named *Massachusetts Professor of the Year* (1994-5) by the Carnegie Foundation and by the Council for the Advancement and Support of Education, Dr. Paul-Emile was honored by the University of Massachusetts, receiving its *Distinguished Scholar Award* and was awarded Bentley University's highest teaching honor: *The Adamian Award for Teaching Excellence.* She is a four-time winner of the *Teaching Innovation Award,* a two-time winner of the *Martin Luther King Jr. Leadership Award,* and the recipient of several publication awards.

She is presently completing manuscripts on the challenges of the mythic heroic path entitled: *Spirit Warrior: Inner Journeys,* a collection of visionary and contemplative poetry, *Soul Keepers* and a critical review of *Slavery and the English Romantic Poets: William Wordsworth, Samuel Taylor Coleridge and Robert Southey.*

Also by Barbara Paul-Emile

Seer

The Dance of Life: Poems for the Spirit

CPSIA information can be obtained at www.ICGtesting.com
Printed in the USA
LVOW11s1954110815

449697LV00008B/715/P